W9-BYU-965
0 00 30 0371161 5

dog

a short novel

by Michelle Herman

dog

a short novel

by Michelle Herman

MacAdam/Cage

MacAdam/Cage Publishing
155 Sansome Street, Suite 550
San Francisco, CA 94104
www.macadamcage.com

Library of Congress Cataloging-in-Publication Data

Herman, Michelle.
Dog : a novella / by Michelle Herman.
p. cm.
ISBN 1-59692-111-0 (hardcover : alk. paper)
1. Human-animal relationships—Fiction. 2. Man-woman relationships—Fiction. 3. Middle aged women—Fiction. 4. Women dog owners—Fiction. 5. English teachers—Fiction. 6. Women teachers—Fiction. 7. Women poets—Fiction. 8. Dogs—Fiction. I. Title.

PS3558.E6825D64 2005
813'.54–dc22

2004030826

Manufactured in the United States of America.
10 9 8 7 6 5 4 3 2 1

Book and jacket design by Dorothy Carico Smith.

For Glen and Grace

The dog, the dog, the dog—the dog had taken over her life.

But this was not necessarily a bad thing. Perhaps she had needed to have her life taken over.

This—a thought on the fly, as it were, as she raced along behind the selfsame dog, the ridiculously expensive leash pulled so taut between them that if she stopped running to keep up with him, she feared the dog would choke to death—made her laugh out loud, and in response the dog stopped suddenly, too suddenly for her to stop, and she nearly tripped over him.

She was a little drunk. No doubt that explained at least some of this. The lament for sure, and possibly the wry judgment on herself. Almost certainly the laugh—a shock of noise to both of them after fifteen or twenty minutes of pure silence but for their footfalls on the sidewalk and the steady jangle of the metal tags that hung from the dog's braided leather collar (his necklace, she called it when she took it off him each night after the midnight walk, so that their clanking wouldn't disturb her sleep: *Here, let me take off your jewelry, darling*), plus her hard and shallow breathing as she did her middle-aged best to keep up with him. Also how close she'd come to falling, to breaking an arm or a leg or spraining an ankle, all because of a dog.

A dog she had never intended to own. The very concept—ownership of a living creature!—dismayed her. As did the concept of caretaking. She lived alone. She did not—it was not in her nature to—*take care.*

A dog she therefore had no business having.

The dog (but he was not even a dog yet but a puppy, just over eleven weeks old) was sitting on the cold sidewalk, considering her. He looked very serious.

"Silly," she said, and bent to pat his head. "It was just a laugh." The dog cocked his head—he looked genuinely puzzled—which made her laugh again.

But this time the sound of her laughter didn't alarm him.

"A human thing," she explained, and oddly enough this seemed to satisfy the dog. He gave a little nod, or what looked to her like a nod (did dogs nod? She knew nothing about dogs), and stood and turned, then abruptly bounded ahead again, yanking her behind him.

Her name was Jill. The dog, unfortunately, was named Phil. She had named him herself. She hadn't noticed (and this was strange, she granted, because she was a poet; you'd think it would have been impossible for her not to have noticed) the rhyme.

Well, it wasn't altogether as strange as it appeared to be. This was what she felt obliged to explain when people asked. To begin with, she had named the dog *Philip*. It had not occurred to her that she would call him Phil. She was not the sort of person who clipped names short. She disliked even the word "nickname." She had never had one herself. She had a name that sounded like a nickname but wasn't—it was the only name she had—and she disliked *it*. "Jill": so girlish, so *truncated*-sounding. So lightweight. Even as a child she had known that she was not a lightweight, that the name didn't suit her. From the time she was ten she had signed her schoolwork "J. T. Rosen."

She had named the dog in a hurry. He had been called Dog—that was the poor creature's name!—by the "foster father" who had been keeping him, caring for him, since rescuing him from the pound. The man was a volunteer for an organization called Fostering Care, which meant, he told her over the phone, that his name was on a list of people who could be called to take in dogs that were about to be "put down," to look after them beyond the pound's two-week limit and try on their own to find permanent homes for them.

He couldn't afford to become too attached to the dogs he took in as "fosters," he said. "I made that mistake the first couple times. Learned pretty fast." Still, a dog had to be called something—sometimes, he explained, he'd have one with him for months before a home was found—and long ago he'd settled on Dog, unless of course he already had another Dog with him when he brought a new one home. Jill considered this. How many dogs had he taken in, then? she wanted to know.

"Geez, who can say. Tell you the truth, I never counted. Hundreds, I reckon."

She had to ask. "What happens if you take in another one after you've named one Dog?"

"Oh, I have four others out in my garage right now that've come in after Dog did. This Dog, the one you're interested in, just so happened to turn up when I had no other dogs here except my own. But two, three days later came Pup, and then—bang—the next week there was Girl, Boy, and Guy. All real nice dogs. You might want to have a look at them too, if you decide to come over."

"How about your own dogs?" Jill asked.

"Oh, my dogs aren't available to be adopted out." He sounded alarmed. "Those are *my* dogs. I keep them."

"No, I mean—I'm sorry—do they have real names?"

"They all have real names." Now he sounded insulted. "Some names are just more…you know, attachment-oriented than others."

Jill was silent, briefly, thinking this over: a man who felt comfortable uttering the words "real nice" and "I reckon" *and* "attachment-oriented."

"That's what I meant," she said. And added, delicately, "Names that suggest you're willing, even glad, to be…attached."

"Oh, yeah, sure. They're Gypsy, Lucky, and Fido—Fido sounds like it's kind of a joke, I guess. But I liked the idea when it came to me. You know, it's so old-fashioned. Not many people name their dogs Fido these days."

"True enough," Jill said. And because he seemed to expect it: "It's a very nice name. They all are."

The man's name, improbably enough, was Bill. She didn't tell people that. They would have made it part of the joke. She tried not to think about it, actually. It made the whole thing seem a bit of a farce.

PERHAPS it *was* a bit of a farce.

Jill had found Bill and Phil (but he hadn't been Phil then, obviously; he had been Dog first—well, not *first*; first, for the five weeks of his life before he was brought to the pound, presumably he had had no name at all—so, first nothing, then Dog, then briefly Philip; now Phil, it seemed, for good) by accident. She had typed "adoption" and "foster" and "home" and the name of the town in which she lived into Google—and it was nothing, it was a lark: late at night, drinking a little wine, putting off going to bed because she knew she wouldn't be able to sleep—and all but one of the ten sites that came up first (out of a possible 1,113 hits in an eleven-second search, Google informed her) concerned dogs and cats, not children. It hadn't crossed her mind that she needed to specify "children" or "human beings" in order to investigate what she wasn't even sure she wanted to investigate—what she was not *investigating* but only curious about, and only mildly and ambivalently, late-night passingly so—but she would be forty-five in less than a year, and it was getting on to two in the morning, and she was drinking Côtes du Rhône and fooling around on the computer, stalling her bedtime, because she hated getting into bed until she was sure she was completely exhausted—at which point she would read in bed for an hour or two anyway—and then what? Was she to spend her middle age, her old age (and then at last to die) alone with her computer and her books and all the *tchotchkes* on the mantelpiece and stacks of students' poems and their half-baked essays about poems, and her own poems still unfinished everywhere about the house, sheets and scraps of paper on her kitchen counter, on the cover of the toilet tank, on her chest of drawers and dressing table and both of her desks, upstairs and down, and all over the rosewood table in the dining room, like snowflakes that refused to melt or fallen leaves with all the color bleached (or leached, or bled) from them after they'd lain too long unraked under the sun—an undergrowth of paper undermining all her efforts to live an orderly and graceful life, to live up to the beauty of the furniture she'd chosen and arranged so carefully in every room of a house in which there was nothing *living* except her, not even a houseplant (because she killed plants; she could not be trusted to recall that plants required water daily) to beckon her home?

It was a morbid turn of thoughts, a late-night impulse, a dread of insomnia, self-pity, curiosity—it was nothing. Still, she wandered into first one and then another of the dog-adoption sites. She wasn't tempted by the cat sites—cats struck her as cliché. Didn't every spinster poet have a cat or two? No, she thought: every spinster legal secretary, bartender, and orthodontist had a cat or two—and she could not tolerate (not even as a lark, not even for a moment at ten minutes before two A.M.) embodying cliché.

She wandered, clicking in and out, sipping her wine, clicking and sipping, and suddenly there was the Fostering Care website (fostercare4orphanpups.com) and photographs were loading, an entire page of them—thirty-two small color photographs of dogs—and she scrolled down to look at all of them and read the lines of type beneath each one. There was "Mocha. Eighteen weeks. Male. Mostly chocolate Lab. Knows some commands. Best in home w/out other dogs or children!" and "Doobie. Three-month-old little girl, cute as a button, spaniel-retriever, gets along with cats. Owner gave up whole litter." "Guinness, 1 yr, 60 lb, Heinz 57 (100% Pure Mutt!!). Will need fenced-in yard. Knows his proximals." And then there was "Dog": Dog with his sad, intelligent, huge eyes, "eyes as big as saucers"—a phrase she remembered from a fairy tale she had loved as a child (the dog guarding something precious; she had forgotten what)—and his black, somber muzzle, his floppy caramel-and-black-striped ears. "Dog. Nine weeks old. About eight pounds. Brindle mixed breed. Found by Good Sam. at five weeks, stray w/out littermates, mother." And then the foster father's name—Bill—and his phone number.

It had all occurred almost without her participation. The website, the photograph, the phone call, the visit—all of it, as if she had been sleepwalking.

She had called Bill first thing in the morning, before she'd even had a cup of coffee, before she lost her nerve, carrying with her the phone number on a Post-it note she'd stuck on the cover of the new *Paris Review*. After she hung up, she dressed quickly and left the house—she hadn't the stomach for breakfast; she wasn't aware of being nervous, exactly (she felt as if she were being propelled forward, just the way she felt as she walked onstage to give a reading of her poems), but she was tense: she was in a state of heightened *readiness*—and without hesitating drove to Bill's house, way across town, stopping only at the Tim Horton's drive-through window for an extra-large cup of terrible coffee.

Then before she knew it, she had a dog in her car beside her, a dog Bill had promised her would grow up to be a "nice medium-sized dog" but right now was the size of a newborn baby, sitting upright and alert on top of a stack of student poems she should have been at home reading on a Saturday morning, and in the back seat the Ziploc bag of kibble Bill had given her to get her started, and the yardlong length of rope he'd knotted onto a cheap collar. "You'll need to walk him later," he called as she headed out to her car with the puppy in her arms, and hurried to hand over the collar and rope-leash. In the right front pocket of her jeans was the list he'd written out for her of everything she'd need. He had even headed it, in neat block letters, WHAT YOU NEED. Collar, leash, food, bowls, toys, treats. "This is just the basics," he said. "Just to get you started. There's other things you'll want to pick up along the way. But this'll do you for now."

"Thank you," she said. "You're a good man, Bill." Suddenly she was embarrassed. "A good person," she emended.

"Shucks," he said. He really did.

Oh, yes indeed: a farce.

OF COURSE, there were times when it *all* seemed rather a farce: the pretty little house of which she was so proud (house-proud!—one of her few vanities; because there were so few, she tried not to hold them against herself) and all the books she'd jam-packed into it: hundreds of books in floor-to-ceiling bookcases she'd had custom-built for every room except the kitchen. Even the foyer and the upstairs hallway—even the bathroom—had been fitted for books. And she'd had good reading light installed in each room too: yielding to a fantasy that dated from her childhood and youth (twenty years in ill-lit rooms, two cramped stories of them, through which she was forever wandering in search of someplace, anyplace, to read) and that had been nurtured for the fifteen years that followed her escape from Flushing to the six-by-nine-foot room in Greenwich Village lit only by three Salvation Army lamps, no overhead—a fantasy, in other words, of a reading paradise.

The house, the many thousand books, the quality and multitude of lights. The *tchotchkes* on the mantelpiece: the glass eggs, the glass flowers in the silver pitcher her grandmother had insisted that she take when she first moved into the single room on Barrow Street that passed for an apartment ("A home of your own! Your first!" her grandmother cried, as she pressed upon her china, wineglasses, soup spoons, and linen tablecloths—as gleeful as her mother was tight-lipped with disapproval), the shells and geodes and beach glass she'd been collecting since her childhood, and the tiny boxes in a multitude of shapes, materials, and colors (wooden, bronze, tin, brass, silver-and-abalone-shell, papier-mâché; squares, stars, rectangles, ovals, crescents, octagons); the framed photographs of her grandmother—gone now for eleven years—and her long-dead grandfather, and her "other grandparents," as she thought of her father's parents, whom she'd never known; and the dozens of saltcellars she had somehow managed to amass over the years, every one of which she superstitiously kept filled with salt. The furniture she'd bought with such purposeful care, one item at a time, and placed in each room with such ceremony, so much thought, so patiently—the same way she wrote her poems, though much more quickly. It had been nine years between her first book, *Fire Escape,* and *In the There-and-Now,* her second. The third was still in progress after eight and a half years—"in progress" something of a euphemism. Stalled, in fact. As thus was her promotion from associate to full professor—for she had been hired, then tenured six years later, on the basis of Great Promise.

The teaching job itself—*teaching* itself, the fact that twice a week a roomful or two of young people hung upon her every word, sometimes even taking notes—and the Promise that had granted her the right to these roomfuls of people, then allowed her tenure. *Tenure!*—the idea of it: a job guaranteed for life. Like a Supreme Court justice, she had told her mother when her brother, Norman, who had taken a straight path to the Academy—college, graduate school, tenure-track job (not to mention marriage, kids, et cetera)—was tenured at *his* institution, well before she was, at hers.

The very fact that both her mother's children, who'd grown up in Flushing in a semi-detached brick in which the only books were *Reader's Digest* Condensed, arranged around the living room in groups of three and four by color, and surrounded by porcelain figures (ladies, dogs, clowns, hoboes), were tenured professors. Professors! These children of the mother who had dropped out of Queens College after one semester to get married (to the father—"a poor orphan," as her mother always said—who had not managed to finish high school, who took the subway from Queens every day into "the city" to an office on the fourteenth floor of a gray building on Tenth Avenue and Thirty-third, while the mother stayed at home "to care for the children"). The fact that her mother, now a widow, lived in Florida and took yoga and low-impact aerobics classes, played bridge every Thursday afternoon and went "disco dancing" with a group of her "girlfriends" on Friday nights, and once a month attended Senior Singles Speed-Dating Soirées—having way more fun at sixty-six, she liked to point out, than her daughter had at "not even forty-five."

When it suited her mother's purposes, Jill was "not even" forty-five. At other times, for other purposes, she was "a woman *your age*" still wearing her hair too long and as unruly as it had been when she was sixteen—"when it was bad enough, but you had an excuse, you didn't know any better"—and no makeup, still no makeup, what could she be thinking, letting herself go, and why not do something about the gray while she was at it, "a nice cut and a little color, nothing too dramatic," it was only natural to take a little care, fifty was *just around the corner*.

That fifty was just around the corner.

No, not a *farce*. Farce suggested satire; farce gave the situation too much credit. Farce was something that could not but make one laugh. She wasn't laughing; who was laughing? It was a situation comedy—what she imagined a situation comedy must be; she wasn't sure she'd ever actually seen one. But her students used them as examples in class all the time. Years ago she'd given up telling them that she had no idea what they were talking about when they referred to so-and-so saying such-and-such on *Seinfeld* or *Friends*—that she hadn't had a TV since she'd left her parents' house, that the last program she'd watched had featured Shari Lewis and Lamb Chop.

Well, it was *her* situation comedy.

The thrust of the situation being that she'd soon be forty-five, with fifty just around the corner, that she was a tenured professor with two volumes of poetry to her name—neither one in print now, but they could be found in libraries, and in boxes in a closet in her office on campus—and a charming wood-frame house, and that her life now boiled down to the care of one small dog.

It was true. All day long now it was feed the dog, take the dog out, where's the dog now?, find the dog a toy to occupy him so he wouldn't lie in the red bergère beside the fireplace staring into space and doing nothing, so she wouldn't feel guilty about ignoring him while she was upstairs working in her study.

And while she worked in her study, while she was thinking, while she was right in the middle of a thought, the dog was as likely as not to come trotting up the stairs and straight to her study and bark once, sharply, letting her know that he needed to go out, and though it took only a few minutes—up out of the chair, down the stairs, leash him up, throw on her jacket and boots, and out the door to lead him to the spot he'd chosen as his favorite, by the dying ornamental cherry tree in the southeast corner—no more than five minutes, really, before she was back at her desk, it was enough to interrupt her train of thought, to irritate her, to leave her muttering and jumpy. She might say something unpleasant to the dog if he followed her back upstairs to her study—"God*damn* it, Phil, get out from underfoot," or "Go away, will you? Must you be so needy?"—and then she'd feel ashamed, and shame derailed her train of thought for good. She berated herself: it wasn't the poor dog's fault that he needed to pee, that he was still a puppy and couldn't hold it in all day. Which was why it didn't work to ask the dog to wait a minute—"Just hang on there, Phil, okay, just give me a second here"—while she tried to pin the thought down after he'd come barking at her. He *would* wait; he wouldn't bark again—she could swear he understood every word she said to him—but would sit there looking grim and even stoic while she scratched pen to paper. How was she supposed to concentrate *that* way? It seemed hideous to be so much at someone else's disposal, seemed wrong to take advantage of her position as the human. The one in charge. In charge—ha! She would put down her pen and take him out. Then she would be angry, then ashamed of herself. And so on.

The dog, the dog, the dog! The time he took! The attention, the energy, the work, the worry. She worried about everything. Whether she was feeding him enough or the right sort of food—and the vet shrugging when she asked him, saying, *Oh, it's all about the same, all those high-priced pet store foods. Pick any one and follow the instructions on the bag, that's all there is to it,* so that she worried about whether she had chosen the right vet.

When she wasn't with the dog, when she was away teaching, the thought of him at home alone would worry her. At first she'd locked him in the bathroom behind a gate she'd bought especially for this purpose, but she hated locking him up when he had lived behind bars for so much of his life, and he was so *good,* so lacking in malice or even mischief, so quickly housebroken, so undestructive, that she began to leave him loose to roam the house as he wished. Loose, but lonely, she feared. Lonely and bored. What did he *do* while she was gone? Sleep. Think. Gnaw a bacon- or a peanut-flavored Nylabone. Chase the rubber Kong packed tight with freeze-dried liver treats nearly impossible to get to (and was that fun for him—"good exercise for mind and body," as the book on dog care had assured her—or was it, as she feared, sadistic?).

He had a cardboard box full of toys that bounced or squeaked, that could be flung and chased or chewed on or fought with. Every time she went to the grocery store—where she had been astonished to discover an entire aisle she'd never before noticed, lined on both sides with items just for dogs to play with—she brought home something else to keep Phil entertained.

She worried about not giving him a good enough home, a home that made up for his early deprivation.

Perhaps it was the worry, not the dog, that was

taking over her life.

Her mother would say—if she admitted this to her mother, which she was not about to do; she hadn't even told her mother she *had* a dog—that it was about time she'd started worrying about something or someone other than herself. Her mother would say, slyly, "Maybe there's someplace you could go with the dog where other single people go with *their* dogs?" Then she would be off again about the singles parties she enjoyed so much, the ten-minute "dates" sitting across a table from one after another "gentleman who was at one time *quite* big in his field," chatting and taking notes until an alarm clock rang, then moving on. "It's very modern, it's the newest thing—I read an article about it." She actually ended up going on real dates with some of these men, retired CPAs and grocers and insurance men and "Les, who was *very* important in the garment industry, and you'd hardly believe he's seventy-seven years old—a lovely man, with gorgeous manners and a beautiful head of hair, still." She'd forget that they were talking about Jill's life, not hers—

she'd be on to her night out dancing with Les, "nice old-fashioned dancing, just lovely, with a big band playing songs I remember from the first time around when I was dating, very nice, the whole band in white dinner jackets," and from there to the fun she'd had with the gals last Friday night ("and there was a good-looking fellow who looked to me younger than myself who wanted to buy us *all* drinks, but we declined, Sydelle told him we were having plenty of fun all by ourselves")—and the next time they talked she might not even remember that there *was* a dog. If Jill mentioned him, her mother would say, "A dog? What's this about a dog? What dog?"

SHE STRODE, she trudged, she stumbled—each in turn—behind the dog. Her bare right hand, clenched around the leash, ached, but she was afraid to change hands, afraid to let go even for a second.

And it wouldn't have helped much in any case. Her left hand, at her side, was frozen and throbbing too. She couldn't keep it in her pocket for long—she was too prepared for the possibility of falling; she wanted to be ready to brace herself, just in case.

Foolish, to have come out without gloves.

It was very cold. It was cold enough so that even though she was somewhat drunk (though she wasn't *that* drunk, she thought—she wasn't, was she?) she could tell how cold it was.

She wondered if the temperature had fallen since she had last taken Phil out in the backyard, after dinner—or perhaps, because they'd been outside for only a few minutes, she simply hadn't noticed then how cold it was.

And she had already been a little drunk then, hadn't she?

At first—just over two weeks ago, when she had brought the dog home—she had tried walking him at seven-thirty or so, following her dinner and his. She had never noticed how many dog-walkers were about at that hour—but then it was possible she had never been outdoors in her own neighborhood right after dinner. That first night, she was amused, and then after a while amazed. Everyone she passed (her neighbors! With whom she had barely spoken in all these years) stopped to comment on the puppy—how cute he was, what lovely markings. And so lively! So sweet! Smart too, wasn't he?

She met Lindsey and Kelsey. Or was it Kelsey and Lindsey? Immediately following the introductions, she forgot which was the dog—a setter mix, a year old—and which was the dog's owner, a cheerful blond girl in her middle twenties. She met Janet and Maggie—Maggie the dog, an elderly retriever who suffered from arthritis; Janet a retired librarian, likewise arthritic, both dog and woman swearing by glucosamine tablets (information Janet volunteered as integral to her introduction)—and Jerry and Valor, Lucas and Sinatra, Daniel and Las Vegas (Sheltie), Bryn and Andanza (Aussie), Stephanie and Snowstar (an Alaskan malamute), and Christopher and Steve and their trio of shiba inus—Ginger, Loki, Balto. And then there were the dogs accompanied by humans who didn't introduce themselves, who only asked Phil's name and introduced their dogs to him. Phil thus met Finnegan and Sally, Sadie, Ruby, Bishop, a huge basset hound named Bumpadeeah, a Renaldo, a Gizmo, a Raven, a Jed. A Tamkin, which made Jill laugh out loud. The owner looked askance at her: *what's funny?* So she didn't ask him, as she wanted to, if the dog had been named for the con man, the doctor and philosopher and amateur poet, in Bellow's novella. It wasn't likely anyway, given Tamkin's owner, a sad sack of a middle-aged man with exhausted-looking eyes, shambling and overweight, a little seedy, she thought—actually, it occurred to her later, not unlike Bellow's protagonist, whose looks had in fact been modeled, she had read, on the poet Delmore Schwartz, so perhaps...well, you never knew. You could never tell who was "literary"—not by something as misleading as looks; you'd think she'd know that much by now.

There was talk among the dog-walkers of housebreaking and crate training, retractable leashes, buckle collars versus slip collars versus Gentle Leads, excessive barking, chewing, Bitter End (a product recommended by Kelsey/Lindsey to discourage gnawing on furniture and leash-grabbing while walking), size and weight and rate of growth, temperament and intelligence, mutts versus purebreds (the walkers of the mutts were the ones who spoke of this, the mutts always coming out ahead), and frequency of bowel movements, which without exception were referred to as "poops."

On the second day, she ventured out to walk Phil in the morning, before breakfast and the Sunday *Times,* and again there was much socializing —a veritable parade of dogs alongside or pulling just ahead of chatty owners. A different crowd in the A.M. Angel, Buddy, Rosie, Foxy, Jackson, Beatrice B., Lance, Elvis, Bridget, Bentley and Mercedes (matching bichons frisés), a one hundred and ninety-pound black mastiff named Big Claude, and a preternaturally calm, off-leash yellow Lab mix named Lakota. In the morning, the dog-walkers wanted to talk about both dog and non-dog matters: the weather, the neighborhood, a smattering of current events (strictly local and statewide), as well as obedience and poops. She was very tired after the walk and had to take a nap; Phil napped with her, in the bed.

And then all day that day, every hour or so—following the advice of a book she'd bought at the pet store when she'd shopped for the supplies on Bill's list—she took Phil into the backyard to relieve himself. The trick to housebreaking, the book explained, was to take the dog out constantly, just for a minute, before he had a chance to "make a mistake," particularly every time he woke from a nap—even just a ten-minute nap—along with his regular daily walks "for exercise and socialization." If one did this for a few days, the book assured her, the dog would get the idea. She took this seriously, and spent her Sunday going in and out of the house. It was halfway through that day that she'd loaded Phil in the car and went out to buy a pair of dog-walking boots. She owned only very good shoes—her boots were Italian, high-heeled; her sneakers were hundred-dollar cross-trainers, which she had no desire to get muddy. Her shoes, like her house, were one of her vanities. Indeed, the single touch of her own taste she allowed in her teaching uniform was in her shoes: her pumps were gorgeous, expensive, very high-heeled. One morning not long ago, a colleague—a full professor in Rhetoric and Composition—smiled at her with closed lips in the elevator and said, "My! Those are quite something! Do women still wear shoes like that?" Jill pursed her own lips and looked down at her feet in pale pink four-inch heels, which matched her perfectly serious-looking pink silk blouse. "Evidently they do," she said.

On that second evening, after dinner, she walked the dog again around the neighborhood. She wore her brand-new boots (All Man Made Materials, ten bucks at Payless), and she didn't chat this time, just smiled at the other dog-walkers, and after Phil had had a good sniff of each dog's bottom, and in several cases a quick wrestle too, she moved on. *But no man moved me till the tide / went past my simple shoe*, she recited silently.

The next day she skipped the morning walk—she was rushing to get to campus, so she just took Phil out back before she left (still thinking of Emily

Dickinson: *I started early, took my dog*), then put him in the bathroom, the gate across its doorway, when she left the house, and came home between classes to take him out in the yard again—and although she walked him for twenty minutes after dinner, she did not at all enjoy it. She decided afterwards that she would not ever again take him out at the Doggy Hour—so she referred to it to Phil, who wagged his tail pensively—and the following night, she watched out the living room window, discreetly, hidden by the dark red curtains she'd had made to match the bergère. She started watching at eight and peeked out intermittently until after eleven. She'd had no idea the Doggy Hour was *hours* long. Dogs of all stripes and their human partners—each of whom delicately carried a knotted plastic grocery bag in the hand not holding the leash—paraded by her house. When two pairs met, they would stop and chat; the dogs would sniff and circle, bark and mount. Leashes tangled. She observed, from this vantage point, a complex range of dog personalities. And human personalities too, as she watched the efforts made by humans to make their dogs behave as they wished them to toward others—in every case, a pointless effort. The dogs were what they were. The humans shrugged—resigned, making apologies—and separated.

After eleven the show was over, the coast clear. By midnight—this was a residential neighborhood in the Middle West, after all—the streets were dead, deserted. It would be their own private Doggy Hour, she told Phil. He could do his business in her small backyard as necessary, and it struck her that this was just as well: she'd never had much use for her backyard before. She was not a barbecuer, not a sit-in-the-sun-in-a-chaise-longuer, not a bird-watcher or a gardener. She did not even write nature poems. She had dutifully, glumly, kept the backyard mowed since buying the house. (Her first summer, she had not mowed. But the grass grew so tall she could not walk through it to the trash cans in the alley; she had to hire someone to come cut it all down, and when he came he shook his head and said, "You could have all manner of rodents living in here, you know," which had horrified her.) But she resented mowing, resented the grass she had no use for. Now she had a purpose for the yard, a reason to mow when spring came this year. Eventually, she thought, she would fence the yard in, so Phil would have a place to play in private. He was hers—as much hers as the child she might someday have thought seriously about adopting, more seriously than she had been "thinking" (she had not been thinking!) about it the night she'd accidentally found Phil—if not by nature then by nurture—*hers*: surely a dog nurtured her way would prefer a private play area to the neighborhood dog run about which she had been told (by Janet, by Lucas, by Stephanie). "Wouldn't you, Phil?" she asked him. "Wouldn't you like to have a place of your own to run around in?"

And in the meantime, they had their midnight walks. Phil had quickly learned to save his energy until then, which pleased her very much. She could not have lived with a stupid dog. And there was no doubt that he wasn't stupid. The intelligent look she had seen in his eyes from the first had not led her astray. He learned things far more quickly than some of her students did.

And he was smarter, it seemed, than other dogs.

Housebreaking, for example, which she had been assured was difficult, had been simple for Phil. He had picked it up in no time, despite everyone's warnings and after only two "mistakes." "Everyone" was her students, the only people she talked to about anything of consequence anymore, and either Kelsey or Lindsey and a number of the other dog-walkers that first night.

"Housebreaking's a bitch," Lucas—in black leather jacket and black jeans and a baseball cap that had B# inscribed on it—told her. "Sinatra's almost two years old and still has accidents." He said this without the least trace of despair but Jill was dismayed. Was one to simply get used to accidents? Were they a fact of life?

No, they were not. The book she had been clever enough to buy at the pet store had told her exactly what to do and she had done it, and in two days the dog was "housebroken." She was rather absurdly pleased with herself about this. She had housebroken a dog! She was a genius! And the dog was a genius too.

She did seriously think sometimes that Phil was a genius of a dog. But perhaps everyone thought this about their dogs. Just as people thought it about their children, and with little more to go on than she had. A child would utter a first sentence—"Dada read book now," as her brother had reported of his firstborn ("Ten months old! And she made absolutely clear what her desires were! It's remarkable!")—and the parents were ready to petition Harold Bloom to add a name to the second edition of his compendium of great minds.

Well, Phil couldn't speak to her but he certainly made his desires clear. This wasn't much to go on—this, and the rapidity with which he'd picked up housebreaking, his understanding that his pleasure walks (for exercise if not socialization) would occur just once a day, after the day was done (and furthermore that forgoing a social life among the neighborhood dogs did not seem to trouble him at all), and the keen, intelligent look in his eyes. The sad but highly intelligent look. Perhaps it wasn't much, but it was enough. After all, he was the only dog she had. It was not permissible—she said this to herself as if it were a joke—for him to be anything less than a genius.

SHE HAD STARTED out as a genius, she reflected as she jogged behind the dog. Or so she had grown up believing. Those test scores! Skipping grades in elementary school and one in junior high. College over and done with before she was twenty. Her mother had been especially proud of this. She still talked about it, as if this—rather than the two volumes of poetry or the various grants and awards or the fact that the daughter, in middle age, was a college professor—were the real measure of her success.

No, it was that the earliest measures of her "success"—the ones that had been measured under her mother's roof—were the ones that counted. Why, her mother had dragged with her to the West

Palm Beach condo for which she had fled Flushing ten years ago (when, in a confluence of tragic events, Jill's father died and Jill left Manhattan for this teaching job; Norman had left the city long ago, left for college—unlike Jill—and never came back) a boxful of Jill's report cards, math tests bearing perfect scores, book reports and "themes" (*How I Know I Am Alive,* by J. T. Rosen).

Her college diploma hung in her mother's den in the condo. "Though I don't see why it doesn't have your real name on it," she had said when Jill told her she was welcome to it.

"This *is* my real name, Mother." She didn't mention how much trouble it had been to make sure her name was inscribed the way she wanted it.

Professionally she had been J. T. Rosen from the beginning. One might say, she supposed, that this began at age ten, when she first published her poems in the grade-school yearbook. Later on, she was Staff Poet, a position she invented, for her high school newspaper. And later still (she was twenty-one; by then she'd been sending poems out in batches of six to quarterlies, picked at random, for years): "Shortcomings, Homecomings," a poem by J. T. Rosen, in *National Poetry Review.*

J. T. Rosen, winner of the American Poetry Series award for a first book (for *Fire Escape*). J. T. Rosen, Associate Professor of English (Creative Writing Workshops, Prosody, Twentieth-Century Literature) and Editor, *The Journal of Middle American Poetry*—another terrible name, but there was nothing to be done about that, and she could not bring herself to refer to it as *J-Map*, as the graduate students she hired each year to help her with it inevitably did. Even if she'd been a fan of acronyms, *J-Map* was too jaunty, no better than "Jill."

People *called* her Jill, of course. But no one she was close to.

Close to! she thought. There was no one she was close to.

PHIL PULLED; Jill followed. She told herself it was a good thing, after all, that she had to keep at a run. If she slowed down, she might freeze to death.

She never dressed herself properly for their walk. She could not seem to *remember* to dress properly for it. She had not once remembered to put on her gloves before she and Phil set out. Not *once*. Nor a hat. What was wrong with her? She had nothing but a T-shirt under her jacket. She should have put on a sweater! Sweatpants over her thin leggings. And socks—why had she not put on a pair of socks?—before jamming her feet into the cheap boots. But she was always forgetting to put on socks to walk the dog, and the Man Made "fur" inside her boots not only did not keep her feet warm but felt sinister against her skin, much worse than something that had once been part of something living—more dead even than that.

They had come to a corner. Before she could even think about which way to go—straight up to Barber Street? Right, to Lang Road?—he pulled her around it, to the left, westward, toward Mosser Road, the one direction she would not have considered, because there was no sidewalk on either side of Mosser, just hard-packed mud and frozen grass. She followed him, however. It was either follow or engage in a tug-of-war, the dog coughing and gasping theatrically as she tried to drag him her way. Why fight, when the stakes were so small?

Why fight indeed?—that was her credo—still, there were times she couldn't keep herself from registering a mild protest. For the record, she thought. Just so the dog would *know* that she was giving in to him, that she had a will too, but was allowing his to prevail. That she had made a choice. Or, perhaps, she thought, less flatteringly, to ask the dog to feel a little sorry for her, to make him see that he was being just a bit of a bully.

She would jog along behind him then, calling, "Don't *tug* so, Phil, take pity on me, will you?"

In reply, he'd speed up, tugging harder.

He was like her this way, she had decided. On principle, he felt obliged to be defiant.

"Phil," she would occasionally call out, just to test him, "don't slow down! Tug harder!" But he didn't fall for it. He forged ahead, dragging her down the street.

And she had to admit, she liked his style. She could not have borne a slavishly devoted dog, a slobberer, a follower, a dog desperate to please her, a dutifully obedient dog begging for approval and affection. Phil was his own dog.

And yet—here was the crux of it, the thing that fascinated and delighted her—he was devoted to her. He adored her. This had been apparent from the moment she had taken him into her arms, in Bill's garage. Bill had had the dog in a cage—he called it a "kennel" but it was a cage, a little prison—alongside other cages of various sizes. Each one held a foster puppy. He opened "Dog's" cage and the puppy scrambled out, straight onto Jill's lap as she knelt on the garage floor. It was as if he were saying, "Ah, it's you! I know you! You're the one I've been waiting for!" She was startled into losing her balance, but even as she tipped backwards the puppy stuck with her, and when Bill gave her a hand so that she could straighten up, the puppy came with her, cradled in her arms.

She stood looking down at him—striped black

on brown, the long black muzzle burrowing under first one of her arms and then the other, then raising his head to look her in the face, gazing into her eyes with his own large, sad, intelligent eyes. They were the same color as hers, nearly black. "Hello, there, Dog," she said, and he licked her cheek. Just once, very precisely—surprisingly unwetly. Then he barked, not loudly. A bark that sounded something like hello. Jill laughed. "He's funny," she said.

"He's taken a liking," Bill said.

"Maybe he's just glad to be out of his…kennel." She was careful; Bill had already corrected her use of the word "cage," told her that it wasn't one, that it was called either a kennel or a crate. "We don't say *cage*." So there were even PC conventions among dog-rescuers.

"Oh, he don't mind it. I let all the foster pups out twice a day to run around in the garage, and about half the time I bring my own dogs out here to chase around with them. They get it all out of their system."

She wondered what "it" was; thought of her own routine: alone at home for hours, days, on end, and twice a week dashing to campus to teach, hours she spent surrounded by people, their needs, their ideas. All that clamor, tumult. The world of others.

She was always relieved to get home again. Glad to have had a little dose of the other, of the great world beyond, but gladder still to be at home afterwards, to change out of her teaching clothes, take off her shoes and jewelry, walk barefoot through the rooms of her own house. She would have to lie down for an hour or two, in silence, in the dark, before she felt herself again. Perhaps Dog felt similarly.

"He's a good dog," Bill assured her.

"I can see that," Jill said. And she felt as if she could.

Well, they'd been right, both she and Bill. Phil was a good dog, an excellent dog. More than that: he was a *complex* dog. He was devoted to her, he depended on her, but once he had settled in at her house—really, by the end of the first day—he had shed his air of the orphanage, shed any trace of neediness, of ordinary dogginess. He seemed to have a stake in not admitting to dependence—in playing it cool. Without enthusiasm he accepted the toy she pressed upon him before she went upstairs to work: a squishy ball, a stuffed baseball bat, a rubber shoe. It was only when she walked away that he deigned to pick it up and play with it.

Even at meal times he would not rush to her, as she imagined any other dog—ordinary dogs—would have done; he would wait until she had set down the food bowl and then slowly, with great dignity, approach it. He would sit down to eat. This gave her more pleasure than it had any right to.

He tolerated her attentions, her baby-talk murmuring, the kisses she planted on his damp black nose. When she returned from campus and said, "Phil! I'm home!" and he came to meet her at the door, he didn't leap up on her, didn't lick or even bark a greeting. He sat down and observed her, coolly pleased that she had made it back again. She could tell he was glad to see her—his tail thumped the floor, giving him away—but he didn't need to prove, to show off, his affection. He valued his coolness; he played hard to get. He didn't want to let her know how much he loved her. Perhaps she would love him less if she knew. Perhaps this was what he thought.

How could she not be charmed?

A dog who pretended his toys were nothing to him, who pretended *food* was nothing to him—indeed, a dog who pretended *she* was nothing to him—how could this be anything but exactly the right dog for her? A dog who did not feel compelled to act like a dog. A dog who was not compelled to simply *be* a dog. A dog with dignity.

For dignity mattered to her; it mattered a great deal. She knew that this amused her students, perhaps even her colleagues; she had been told that the staff found it hilarious. A work-study student who helped with photocopying in the English office had felt honor-bound to tell her that the department secretaries referred to her as Her Royal Highness. Foolishly, Jill had told the student, "That could be any one of us, could it not?" and the earnest girl said, "Oh, no, Professor Rosen, they do an imitation of you that goes with it."

It was hard to say what had earned her this epithet—her bearing, or her speaking voice (she had been told by students that she sounded like she was reciting poetry when she was reading out their homework assignment), or something of which she herself was not aware.

"You don't really seem like a dog person," one of her students had said after she told her advanced prosody seminar that she had adopted a puppy. "Well, naturally not," she said, and the kids all laughed. But she hadn't meant it to be funny. She couldn't say why they so often found her funny.

She couldn't say, for that matter, exactly why her colleagues found her so queer—queer in the old-fashioned sense (they would have been respectful, she imagined, not amused, if they had thought her queer in the new-fashioned sense). It was possible that because she was the only "creative writer" on the faculty—the only official one, the only one who had been hired *as* a "creative writer" (there were several dabblers who resented this, she knew)—they felt it was their duty as legitimate professors of English to be amused by her. Because she told her students on the first day of class that they were expected to address her as Professor Rosen, *never* Jill; because she would not play in the annual students-against-faculty softball game; because she dressed for teaching in what she considered appropriate professorial clothes—her uniform: a gray or black wool skirt, a blouse with every single button done up and a cardigan or blazer over that, a strand of pearls, hose, pumps; because she never went out drinking with her students, and politely, firmly, changed the subject when they dropped in during office hours and began to speak of their personal problems; because she would not share *hers* with them—because the closest she had ever come to personal revelation was her announcement (an impulse she was later sorry she had given in to) that she'd taken in the dog—because of all of this, she supposed, people thought she was peculiar.

Dignity was out of fashion; of what use was it? Like any old-fashioned virtue, it was easy to make fun of. But she had faith in decorum, in seemliness, in vigilance, in seriousness of purpose and affect. And why not, if it helped to banish foolishness and laxity, meaninglessness, worthlessness? Were they in favor of *these* qualities? In favor of *in*dignity?

Down Mosser, past Pearl, past Hagan, a dead end, and a right on Fountain, where there were sidewalks, thank God. The wind whipped her hair behind her as Phil yanked her around the corner and bounded up Fountain, a street named for a family that still lived around here, she'd been told by one of her dog-walking neighbors who actually lived on Fountain and said she was a distant relative of "the original Fountains." The way the woman had talked about them—"an important family, *extremely* big in real estate and also *major* art collectors" (there was a wing named for them in the little art museum downtown: the Beatrice B. and Louis D. Fountain Wing, in which hung the work of long-dead local and other Midwestern artists)—reminded Jill of her mother talking about her dates. The neighbor had named her cocker spaniel Beatrice B., in homage.

The indignity of the "name" Dog—that's what she was thinking of when she hastened to come up with a name for Phil as he sat beside her calmly in the front seat on the way home from Bill's. She hadn't been planning to get a dog, so she hadn't been thinking of names. She had had no time to think. Unlike her mother, who had had months to come up with her idiotic name (*both* of her idiotic names: the "T" was for Terri, which was as bad as—no, really, it was worse than: consider that "i" ending—her first name). But her mother had no knack for making such choices. Her younger brother was Norman Stephen. *Norman Stephen Rosen*: as if she had *tried* to think of three names that would sound ungainly strung together (the repetition of the "schwa-n" sound awful enough on its own, but in trochaic trimeter? Was it so much beyond her resources to summon up a dactyl to replace the middle trochee?). And her mother had had *years* to contemplate a name for the second child she knew she wanted and then knew was coming! (And she *had* contemplated: if Norman had turned out to be a girl, her mother had told Jill, he would have been *Nancy Sharon.*)

When Jill brought the dog home from Bill's and took him upstairs, set him on her bed, and then collapsed beside him—for she felt he needed a nap after his ordeal; so did she, after hers—what she was thinking was that she could not even for a moment bring herself to use the common noun as if it were a proper one. The poor creature was already getting used to *Dog*, which wouldn't do. And there happened to be four books on her nightstand by writers named Philip. She was in the middle of all of them. For years she had slept poorly, and she would read this way—a bit of one, a bit of another—until she was sleepy (sometimes it took several hours, with two or even three dips into each book).

Larkin, Roth, Lopate, Levine. So she named the puppy Philip, after this coincidence, and thought *There, now that's done.*

It wasn't until the next day, as she was pouring kibble into the dog's bowl, drinking her first cup of coffee, that she remembered that there had once been a Philip in her *life*, not just in books. The four books on her nightstand—that was true enough, and it was what she offered when people asked about the dog's name, when they smiled and said, *Really? Jill and Phil? How cute,* but it was just as true, she realized and then afterwards could not unrealize, that she'd once had a lover ("lover" was perhaps dignifying the relationship with a more glorious title than the failed romance deserved; it was a relationship that was almost adolescent in its overall stupidity) whose name had been Philip.

This was long ago—long enough so that no one she knew would know, no one in this Midwestern town she'd lived in for ten years and none of the small number of people in New York with whom she still kept in holiday-card/forward-an-e-mail-petition touch. At least twenty years ago. Still, it irritated her that *she'd* forgotten, or suppressed, this information. "Forgotten" implied that she had had so many lovers she could not keep track of them, which was absurd—but "suppressed" was not her style: she prided herself on the close contact she maintained with her own unconscious. She was the sort of person who had literal-minded dreams: a boat pulling away from a dock as she stood, panting, her suitcase in hand, having Missed the Boat; falling flat on her face when she tripped over a log that blocked her path; standing before a bush studded with sparrows and holding one in her cupped hand.

But indeed, she realized then, the dog reminded her of Philip, that other Philip, forgotten or suppressed when she so hastily named her dog for the four Philips whose books were by her bed. Named him Philip, then began almost at once to call him Phil. She could not say why, or how, this had begun, and now she had no choice—it was the name he answered to. Just as she answered to Jill.

Philip the first—as she now thought of him—had eyes too that suggested both a deep, far-ranging intelligence and bottomless, inconsolable grief (no matter what *she* did or said, and in those days she had done and said much). About Philip the first there was the air of tragedy even in repose; she had never known what was responsible for it. It was possible that he had cultivated it, that he had chosen tragedy—unlike Philip the dog, whose sad eyes had been come by honestly.

The end effect was the same, however: it was impossible to look into either Philip's eyes and remain unmoved.

The first Philip had been, like her, a poet. Unlike her, he had not yet begun to publish his poems in those days. Perhaps this had played a part in the tragedy, she thought now. At the time she had been too callow to consider it. She was younger than he, by five or six years—a gap of nothing much in middle age, but in one's twenties significant. She was twenty-one when they started dating (insofar as they were "dating": they never *went* anywhere together) and they were together (also not quite the right word, since they maintained separate residences—his near Brooklyn College, where he was in graduate school, and hers in the Village, that studio on Barrow Street—and broke up on the average of once a month) for just over a year, a year during which half the poems in what would eventually be her first book appeared in quarterlies and Philip published nothing. As he had continued to do (to not do) in the years, the decades since, she had to assume, as she had never come across a poem of his, and she kept up; she read everything that was worth reading.

She had lost touch with him immediately upon their final break-up, a highly dramatic one that involved shopping bags full of his belongings, which had accumulated in her studio apartment, being dragged through Manhattan and deposited by Jill in the East Village apartment of a friend of Philip's, a short story writer she suspected had a crush on him and was glad to see her out of the picture.

Soon afterwards she left New York for Iowa, and although she thought of Philip then—for it had been he who'd urged her to go back to school, to get an M.F.A., which she had been resisting (had Baudelaire gone to grad school? Had Yeats? Had Elizabeth Bishop? That was her argument in those days. Well, she was in her early twenties—that was her excuse)—she thought it best not to contact him. And she never had, nor had he, her. And all the years had passed.

She wondered if he'd followed her career. And disliked herself for wondering.

She allowed herself to imagine for a moment what he would make of it if he heard somehow that she had a dog she had named Philip.

He would not believe that it had been an accident.

She tugged on Phil's leash impatiently. He had stopped to sniff at the mud-smeared tire of a Volvo station wagon. "Phil?" she said. "A tire? Please." The dog ignored her; he was concentrating. Sometimes she had the feeling he was taking notes—studying, memorizing. "I'm freezing. Could you snap it up? Perhaps a little?" He looked over his shoulder at her—briefly, distractedly—*Can't you see I'm working here?*—and then turned back to the task at hand.

She grinned. She couldn't help it. He *was* like her, wasn't he? And honestly, if she were cold, it was her own fault and not the dog's. She should never have come out at midnight in mid-February without putting on a hat, without her gloves, without warm pants. A sweater over her Poetry Society of America T-shirt. Socks.

"All right, boy," she said. "That's fine. You just take your time, Phil."

The first Philip, she reflected as she waited for the dog, had never been called Phil. Thus the matter of Jill-and-Phil—its terrible, its shameful, its prosaic cuteness—had never come up.

Like Jill, Philip the first had not been the sort of person one would think of calling by a shortened version of his name. What sort of person would that be? she asked herself now, watching Phil inspect the patch of frozen grass and mud along the curb, committing it to memory.

Perhaps not the most pleasant, most approachable, most human sort of person.

It was possible that this was why she had begun almost at once to call the dog Phil. To make sure *he* was approachable. To humanize him.

So here was something else that made her laugh. Another loud, alarming laugh like a gunshot in the silence. But this time it did not disturb the dog, who was quick to adjust to her surprises, whatever they might be. Besides, she had explained herself.

This time Phil merely stopped his studies for an instant to cast a look up at her. *Human*, his look seemed to say. *What a stupid thing to be.*

IN THE MORNING as she drank her coffee and ate half a package of the four-dollars-a-box raspberries she had allowed herself on her last trip to Kroger (she allowed one overpriced indulgence each trip: fresh berries or cherries in winter, artichokes to steam at two dollars apiece, canned hearts of palm, lump crabmeat; a bottle of wine that cost more than thirteen dollars counted too, so she tended to keep her wine purchases on the low end), as Phil sat at his bowl in the corner working his way through his All-Natural Lamb and Rice puppy kibble, she found herself again—or still—thinking of Philip the first. *Still*, she supposed, because she'd dreamed of him last night. In the dream, she had tried to phone him—first from home, then from her office (both phones failing to connect), then from a cell phone (which in life she didn't own) while driving (which she'd never do; she was still a nervous driver, having learned in her mid-thirties), then from a public pay phone, which was broken. Finally standing on the street (the street where she had lived, all those years ago) and calling out to him, without a phone, "I am trying to summon you, goddamn it!"

There was something else about the two—the human and the dog—that she had failed to account for, it occurred to her this morning.

The human Philip, although he had depended on her, clearly couldn't manage without her—he used to phone three, four, five times a day: from home, from a pay phone on the Brooklyn College campus between classes, from his friends' apartments; he wanted to see her every evening and was insulted when she said no, which she felt obliged to do on principle occasionally; he demanded that she read everything he wrote before he sent it out, and he read aloud each draft of every poem to her—had nevertheless refused to admit this dependence; he never spoke of love. He was not affectionate, not the sort of boyfriend who would take her hand or hug her. He was studiously casual toward her, in word and deed. He would call her on the phone—he'd call *her*—and then behave as if she had interrupted him at work. "So what's up?" he'd say impatiently. He'd come to see her and then ignore her, listen to her records (and complain about the selection) or read, sometimes looking up to read aloud to her, and never mind if *she* were reading something then herself, or he'd work on his poems. He'd look at her blankly when she asked a question—"Should we order dinner in? Chinese? Or make spaghetti?"

But like the dog, who after their long walk every night would at last give up his pretense of detachment and curl up with her in bed, lay his head upon her shoulder or her leg, and close his eyes and go to sleep beside her with a series of contented sighs, the human Philip had clung to her in the night.

This had infuriated her. That the dog was cool toward her all day and evening and then broke down and gave himself over to true feeling when he was about to go to sleep did not displease her—on the contrary, it delighted and charmed her (ah, at last! she'd think, you silly dog, so *here* you are)—but what was delightful in a dog was not likely to be delightful in a human being.

Even if Philip's clinging to her in his sleep had not kept her awake, the aggressive shift from distance to closeness that occurred at bedtime would have made her angry. At eleven or eleven thirty, he was still aloof; at midnight, as if a bell had rung and Cinderella's ball gown had melted away, she seemed to become something else to him, someone he was suddenly not ashamed to care for. He required her at night: first for sex and then for sleeping—*his* sleeping, not hers. His arms were so tight around her, one long leg flung over hers, she couldn't sleep. It was the beginning of her insomnia, that year with Philip. Even on the nights he didn't stay with her, she couldn't sleep—on those nights when he returned to Brooklyn to his own apartment, sulking because she'd said no, he couldn't spend the night for once, or because she hadn't let him come see her at all—she was too upset about the conversation they had had about her "banishing" him: "You're cold, you're stone, you have no feelings," he would say, his tone light, teasing. "Isn't that the truth? That you have no heart? You can't write poetry if you have no heart, you know."

Aloof or mean. Those were his two modes with her. Or else asleep, devoted.

You're the one who can't write poetry, she thought. *You're the one. See how it turned out?*

She must have said it out loud. Philip the second looked up from his food bowl, cocked his head.

"It's nothing," she told him. "Don't mind me."

And he shrugged—she could have sworn he shrugged—and returned to his breakfast.

SHE HAD A CLASS to teach this morning—her advanced undergraduate workshop. A good group, thirteen earnest youngsters, some with talent. Not much younger than she'd been when she'd known Philip.

She supposed that he must have taken up something else eventually, must have given up poetry. As she sat down at the seminar table and shuffled the poems that they would talk about today, she tried to picture him doing something, anything, other than sitting with a pen and a notebook, frowning, looking tragic and brilliant. And pretty—for he had been that too, with his long black hair and black eyes (like hers, like Phil the dog's) and long black eyelashes. He'd been tall and slender and graceful and gloomy. He'd *looked* like a poet, like a child's idea of what a poet was meant to look like. She remembered thinking that on the night they'd met, at a poetry reading at the 92nd Street Y. They happened to be sitting next to each other and both of them had been alone, both of them clutching tatty second-hand hardcover copies, dog-eared and much written in, of the poet's books, hoping to get them signed. Not even the poet on stage looked more like a poet than Philip did.

She could not imagine him working in a bank, an office, carrying a briefcase, selling life insurance, driving a taxi. She could not see him any way other than the way he'd been more than twenty years ago, when she had imagined that she loved him. He had made a big impression on her; she was young enough then so that despite her argument against graduate school she was impressed by the way he spent his days and what he knew. He took classes with John Ashbery. He spoke knowledgeably about little magazines—it was thanks to him that she began to publish so many of her poems, really, since he directed her toward the quarterlies most likely to be receptive to her work. Until she'd met him, she'd been sending poems out scattershot, and almost certainly to the wrong places, examining the magazines that she could not afford to buy at the Eighth Street Bookstore and writing down addresses on a memo pad. Philip knew the things she didn't know.

And he read his poems aloud beautifully—read *her* poems aloud beautifully too, better by far than she did even now, even after all these years of giving readings. Philip with his beautiful face, his beautiful black hair, in a black sweater and corduroys and cowboy boots reading poems aloud, talking abou poetry and what it meant to be a poet. How Philip had loved the *idea* of being a poet! And she had loved, she knew, the idea of Philip.

Her students took their places at the table, greeting one another, greeting her—"Good morning, Professor"—shyly, nicely. Sweet-faced children with their thick-soled shoes and turned-back baseball caps, their studded noses, lips, and eyebrows, emitting their clouds of patchouli, setting manuscripts and books down on the table, digging in their backpacks for pens, unscrewing caps from bottled water, snapping Diet Coke tabs, clearing nervous throats.

She had been very young then, with Philip; almost nothing had happened to her yet. Only her family had happened to her, and a few young men, most notably Philip himself. She had not yet left New York—she had never left New York, not even for two weeks of summer camp; she had never traveled anywhere. She had lived at home in Flushing with her parents and her little brother all her life until a year before she had met Philip, lived at home through college, commuting to CCNY although her mother had pushed Queens College ("Why travel so far on the subway every day? Why shouldn't Queens College be good enough, right here in Flushing?"). She was still full of wonder when she looked around her at her own apartment, a closet of an apartment, with the tub in the kitchen and the "kitchen" nothing but the quarter of the room where wood floor yielded to linoleum, where there was a stovetop and a mini-fridge and two shelves above the little square of sink. At the room's other end there was a toilet in the corner, with a shower curtain semi-circling it, and between the two—"bathroom" and "kitchen"—she had set a little desk, a chair, a narrow bed, three ugly, rickety, but serviceable floor lamps, and her brick-and-board shelves, which housed what had seemed to her at that time a great many books. She hung her clothes on hangers hooked around twelvepenny nails she'd hammered here and there into the walls.

She was eking out a living then by proofreading,

temp-typing, and from time to time a little freelance writing. The first jobs she had after graduation—she tried waiting tables for two days, selling clothing for a week; she spent almost a month as a Swiss investment banker's secretary—didn't suit her. She could not bear the indignity of being given orders of any kind: for food, for a bigger size, for a phone call that had to be placed immediately. Later she would find that teaching was the only work for pay that truly suited her, since it did not require her to take orders from anyone.

She could picture Philip, come to think of it, teaching. He had been a sort of teacher to her, back then—lecturing her about going back to school and about where to send her poems, stern about what she hadn't read and had no interest in reading—and he took such pleasure in performance (the aspect of her teaching job to which *she* was suited least). She could imagine him teaching high school English, declaiming poetry to his rapt students, the girls falling in love with him (even if by now, at over fifty, he had lost his prettiness, he would still be handsome, she was sure). Or perhaps he really had given up poetry altogether and turned to something unexpected, something completely different—history, philosophy, science. She could see him in a lecture hall, four hundred heads in rows all looking at him. The kind of class, thank God, she didn't have to teach. It would terrify her. But Philip had so loved an audience. *She* had been his audience, back then.

AFTER HER morning class she had lunch with a colleague, a woman who was writing a book on domesticity in the eighteenth-century novel. She was named March—a name Jill admired, and she wondered if March had chosen it herself, abandoning a birth name, Marcy or Marjorie or even Mary (though Jill herself would have been grateful enough for Mary—Mary or Jane or Ann—a simple, plain, old-fashioned, solid name), or if her parents had been clever and sophisticated, but she didn't know her well enough to ask the question. She didn't know her well enough to be sitting across a table from her, for that matter, but March had invited her.

They exchanged small talk about the progress of their work. Jill was as vague as possible without being rude. She hated to talk about what she was writing or how—or worse yet, why—she was writing it, but March asked. For her part, March was decidedly tedious on the subject of Robinson Crusoe and Friday, and on "the non-domestic spaces that always turn out to be the most domestic of all"—although it did pass through Jill's mind as she sat listening and picking at her salad, worrying just a little bit about Phil, all alone at home, that *Friday* would have been an excellent name for him, that perhaps she should not have settled quite so quickly on Philip. March spoke of an article she was writing—"a bit of a break from the island," she said with a laugh that struck Jill as entirely forced—on cause-and-effect in the novels of Richardson and Fielding.

"A fertile subject," Jill remarked, insincerely. But what was she to say? That it was hard for her to conceive of a more *obvious* subject than cause-and-effect in the novels (or the life, if it came to that) of anyone?

"Of course, my agenda would be at least in part to demonstrate how contingency and domesticity, the two great obsessions of the eighteenth century, are integrally related."

"Of course," said Jill.

March then made some mention of Aristotle ("who, as you know, I'm sure, implies the necessity of cause in his discussion of the laws of probability and necessity") and Jill nodded—*oh, yes, of course*—but at last she moved on: first, to a graduate seminar she was thinking of proposing for next year in "Kantian ethics and the eighteenth-century British novel," and then to an undergraduate class in critical theory she was teaching this term, and how much difficulty some of her students were having ("You know the way they'll look at you sometimes, alarmed and uncomprehending and bored all at the same time? As if you were criminally insane, speaking in a foreign language, *and* failing to produce the rabbit they were hoping was hidden in your hat, all at once?"—and at this Jill almost laughed, despite herself, but when March went on, "It's feminist theory in particular that seems to be their bête noire," it was only a yawn she had to restrain), and finally March took up the subject of the committee assignment she and Jill were to share this spring, the newly formed Committee for Teaching Excellence.

Ah, Jill thought: of course. The mystery of the lunch invitation explained. It had certainly taken long enough. She drank her coffee and listened dutifully, agreeing to everything March suggested. March, who did not yet have tenure, took such things—committees, meetings, memo-writing—very seriously. Just as seriously, it seemed, as she did graduate course proposals, her undergraduates' confusion about feminist approaches to literature, and "ideas of causation." She had no idea that the committee would meet weekly and make plans and make notes and write up those notes and distribute them as memos to the faculty (March would take it upon herself to type everything up and make copies and put them in everybody's mailboxes) and absolutely nothing would come of it. She'd learn. There was no point in telling her; no one ever believed it. She'd find out for herself soon enough. It was a rite of initiation, Jill thought. Just one of many. Welcome to the Academy.

She was ashamed of the little flare of bitterness she felt rise in her throat. Bitterness because March Harris wasn't interested in her? That this lunch invitation had had nothing to do with friendship or even curiosity about her? That there was not even to be a pretense of friendship, that she *had* no curiosity about her?

When she had first begun this job, had moved from New York City to the Midwest, she had imagined that she would be among friends always. It pained her now to think of this. She had imagined a world in which people spoke of, thought of, nothing but books—in which there would be cocktail parties where people drew their heads together close to talk about a new poem in *The Nation,* the new book by Robert Hass, the miracle of Bishop; where they would quote Berryman, make arcane jokes that featured Pound or Joyce, press brand-new novels upon one another ("You must read this at once! And call me, no matter how late, and tell me what you think!"), exchange lists of favorites, desert-island books, the books you knew you had to reread at least once before you died.

It made her blush, remembering.

Instead she learned at once that books were their business; they were eager to be free of them once the workday was donc. No one read living writers, not by choice—even the twentieth-century specialists preferred the dead—and the dead ones had been talked to death in class; what else was there to say? They knew what they thought and they were sick of it.

The talk at parties, start-of-the-year and end-of-the-year picnics, hallway kaffeeklatsches, always, was of departmental politics and "service"—complaints about this committee or that, gossip about who was slacking off—and teaching loads, students, and deans. There was non-academic conversation too, about movies and football, golf, vacations, real estate.

No one spoke of literature; no one spoke of anything one could consider "personal." For her, these categories were essentially the same; she should not have been surprised by one, given the other.

In the end, she had become acquainted with dozens of people. But she had not made a single friend.

She should not have expected to, of course. Her disappointment had in fact caught her off guard, for she had not imagined she was even vulnerable to the wish for friendship anymore. What she was, she decided, was nostalgic—reflexively, meaninglessly nostalgic—for the friendships of her youth, the friendships of the days before she had a *profession*, before ambition, before the Sturm und Drang of boys and men. It was not real longing, was not something she wished to return to. She remembered such friendships the way she remembered writing her first poems, in her careful pre-cursive penmanship on sheets of yellow paper lined in blue and half the size of ordinary paper. She remembered "best friends" with the same kind of distant, useless fondness with which she recalled the basement of her elementary school (the red painted circle around which the girls in her class stood, each with one hand extended, waiting to be smacked, for a game of skip tag) or the Half-Moon ride that was anchored to a truck and came around the neighborhood on summer nights, or playing school with Norman (she the teacher, naturally, and he—age three, or four—her captive student) or eating Carvel ice cream (Brown Bonnet cones!) walking down the street with her father, just the two of them—one of the few memories she had of herself alone with him ("What do you say we leave Mama and your baby brother at home and take a stroll?" She remembered the delicious word *stroll*, and the way he had waved off her mother's objections. How old was she then? Five? Six? She was able to read well enough to be in charge of reading out loud the entire menu: her father said he liked the sound of her voice telling him what all their choices were. "All right," he'd say, and close his eyes to listen, "let me have it"—even though when all was said and done they always ordered the same thing).

It was not as if she hadn't had a friend once she'd left childhood. She'd had friends throughout her youth, through all the various stages *of* her youth: past childhood and adolescence, into college and her early twenties in the Village, and during graduate school, when it seemed to her that she had more friends than she knew what to do with—an illusion fostered by life in a town so small it was impossible to go to the Laundromat or shop for groceries without running into her fellow poets. But afterwards, when she returned to New York City, she kept in touch with no one who had been her "friend" in graduate school. And back in New York? Hardly anyone she'd known before was still there—they'd scattered as distantly and randomly as if someone had shaken them and sprinkled them out over a map—and the ones who hadn't jumped into the shaker, who were still there, had all changed their lives, had proper jobs or started law school or were married or were living with their boyfriends uptown in bigger apartments vacated by first wives.

But even before she'd left for Iowa *she* was changing. She didn't blame her friends—her former friends. Ambition had set in; love had set in. Looking back, it seemed to her that by the time she had become involved with Philip—Philip the first, Philip the human—she had no friends anymore of the kind she'd had before. *Before* meaning before she'd called herself a poet: when she had written poetry simply because she *did*, because it was as natural to her as breaking into a run when she was excited, full of energy on her way home from a long day of second grade, or weeping when her feelings had been hurt at recess, or slamming shut her bedroom door and shouting past it to her mother, "Just leave me alone! You don't understand *anything*, so don't even try!" She'd moved on sometime during college, moved on without knowing it.

It had been nothing but nostalgia—fruitless, random, firing-of-electrons nostalgia—that had set her dreaming when she'd left New York for this job, for what she imagined would be A New Life. She hadn't thought about how long it had been since she'd last had a real conversation with anyone, or about the last friends she'd had in New York—the old altered, crippled friendships, the broken-off bits of friendships, the leftovers of friendships; or the new ones, marked and undermined by a constant rumbling low-grade rivalry of one kind or another, friendships that had been made at a shallower depth anyway, so that when the waves of competition came along, the friendships were knocked off their feet. Friendships formed at the shore. Wading friendships.

The fact was, she could not remember the last truly satisfying conversation she had had with anyone.

Her students tried occasionally to talk to her. But the gulf was enormous, unbridgeable. They were twenty-five years younger than she; they had parents her age. (But the gulf between herself and their parents would be unbridgeable too. It wasn't just a matter of years; it was a matter of realms. When these grown children quoted their mothers and fathers—solemnly or mockingly, it made no difference—Jill held herself still, expressionless. The children, she was sure, had no idea how often this occurred, how often they told her, "My father always says ____________," or, "My mother thinks ____________"; no idea, certainly, how what their parents "always said" or thought—or watched or read or did—dismayed and shocked Professor Rosen.)

The children, her students, lived in their own realm, one so remote from hers she wasn't even clear on its terrain, except that it included television, certain movies, and "text-messaging." Their pop music and drinking habits were unfathomable to her (as no doubt hers would be too, to them); their habitual turns of phrase were puzzling and seemed to her forced, self-conscious, silly (ditto, she was certain).

It was not that they disliked her; not at all. She was aware—they made it her business to be aware—that they rather liked her. They nominated her each year for the department's Superlative Teaching Award and wrote glowing assessments of her classes. And they treated her, always, with amused respect. Indeed, they treated her with a kind of deference that made friendship impossible. They didn't know her; they couldn't know her. It wasn't her job to let them know her. What would be more pathetic than friendship with one's young students?

Oh, she knew what would be more pathetic. Exactly what she had allowed herself to dip a toe into today. To make an effort to have friendships of the truncated, superficial kind that might be offered by one of her colleagues. Not *friendship,* but a meal, a drink, a cup of coffee, a conversation about nothing. She had participated in this ritual when she had first arrived. But it was not for her. Really, she could not see why it was for them. Why did they bother? When they could be working, reading, thinking. They weren't interested in one another; they made no effort to know one another. They behaved as if there were nothing to know, nothing to be known.

It was a transitory, meaningless, instinctive groping, she thought now—this vague hope she hadn't even known had stirred in her when March Harris e-mailed her an invitation out to lunch. March Harris was not someone she was interested in; she had forgotten that. There was no one she was interested in.

The check arrived and March reached for it, saying, "I'll get this one, all right?" Jill didn't argue, although she had planned to. And the implied "you'll get the next one" could be left alone as well; there was no need to comment on what wasn't said.

She had planned to insist on paying for the lunch herself—as a senior colleague, it seemed appropriate—but now she thought, Let *her* buy lunch, why not? She knew for a fact that March, still untenured, hired just three years ago, earned more than she did. "Salary compression," they called it. March, when hired, had been a "most desirable candidate," offered the high end of the range for a new assistant professor. Jill, when she was hired, had been desirable too, but salaries were much lower then, and she had not fulfilled her promise; the raises each year had been meager.

"Thank you for lunch," Jill said.

"It's my pleasure, Jill," said March.

March's name, Jill thought, reconsidering it, was not the best choice, really—not when paired with her surname. It was a hard bridge to cross—the "ch" into the "ha"; still, it was adventurous, imaginative, smart. The allusion to the March Hare was almost too witty. She nearly went ahead and asked, as they walked back to their building, what the Harrises had done—*did*, probably; March was a good ten or twelve years younger than she, and her parents could well be in their mid-fifties—for a living, but she kept that impulse in check. March was talking, as they crossed the campus, about her chances for a Special Research Assignment next year, and her plans to apply for both a Seed Grant and a Grant-in-Aid. What did Jill think her chances were? As good as anyone's, Jill told her. She spoke courteously, coolly: there was no place between them for the personal (and if a place were to be made before they parted, Jill thought, it surely wasn't she who'd make it).

At the threshold of the Humanities building they said their goodbyes. "Thanks again," Jill said.

"Goodbye" alone would have sounded brusque, would have revealed too closely what she felt. And March said, "Sure. It was fun. Let's do it again sometime."

Alone in her office, her head in her hands, fifteen minutes left before her second class, Jill thought about this—"it was fun"—in the context of the dreary hour she had just spent. Imagine what Phil would think if she were able to explain the concept of "fun" to him. Humans—stupid, stupid humans. That was what he'd think.

"Professor?"

A student hovered in her doorway. She straightened up, set her hands flat on her desk. "Yes? What can I do for you, Emily?"

"Are you all right?" Emily looked as if she doubted it, and as if she were about to flee.

"Of course," Jill said. "Don't be silly. And don't *hover*. Come in."

"Only if you're sure I'm not interrupting you. I could come back after class. Or I could just wait till—"

"It's fine. Come." She waved the girl into her office.

Emily wanted to talk about a villanelle she was writing. "It's way harder than I thought," she said.

"Ah, yes, everything is, isn't it."

Emily looked startled. Then she said, "I guess so," and laughed, but with such hesitancy Jill felt sorry for the girl. It was clear she couldn't tell how she was supposed to take her, whether she was allowed to find this funny or not. Jill sighed. Her students, as much as they seemed to like her, were always so *mystified* by her.

As she talked Emily through the intricacies of the villanelle—and, while she was at it, made sure the girl had a handle on each of the other forms on the list she'd handed out on a typed sheet last week (asking them to choose two out of ten and write "essentially the same poem, two ways, to see for yourself what form does: like God, it will give with one hand and take away with the other")—she caught herself thinking of Phil, at home on the bergère. Dozing. Thinking whatever a dog thought.

Dog-thinking. Waiting for her.

She hadn't mentioned the dog to March, she realized—hadn't breathed a word of his existence. She was glad of that, at least.

HER AFTERNOON class—the prosody seminar—and then the grocery store (red leaf lettuce, three overpriced but splendid-looking portobello mushrooms, two bananas, a pint of plain nonfat yogurt, a quart of skim milk, a small package of chicken breasts, a ten-dollar chardonnay, and a rolled-up rubber newspaper that squeaked); then home to the dog. To his yawning, leisurely greeting that didn't fool her. A quick trip to the backyard to let him pee at length. The wine opened and poured, the chicken and the mushrooms cooked in a cast-iron pan with olive oil and herbs and a splash of wine from her glass, a salad made and dressed. Dinner for them both, another glass of wine, another trip to the backyard (one during which she was just a little irritable, since it took Phil forever to find the perfect spot), then an hour of reading in the living room, on the méridienne, across from where Phil, after taking a polite bite and admiring the squeak of his rubber newspaper, took his after-dinner nap on the bergère.

He slept in his chair and she curled up in hers with the Lopate that had been by her bed two weeks ago—*Against Joie de Vivre,* a book she had been meaning to read for years, and that she had taken from the bedstand stack when it became clear that her days of reading in bed were over. Each night now, after the long walk around the neighborhood, not to mention the glass or two of wine beforehand, she was too sleepy to read for even a few minutes, and with Phil beside her in the bed she fell asleep—for perhaps the first time in her life—without difficulty, immediately. Even in the years before her insomnia had begun, even in childhood, she had needed to read in order to sleep. Now the dog took the place of her books in her bed.

But she found now that she was reading more in other places, other rooms, at other hours.

Tonight, after an hour with the Lopate in the living room, she moved upstairs to the armchair in her study, carrying her wineglass and both *The Mercy* and *The Counterlife,* which she'd likewise removed from the bedroom more than a week ago. She had also brought Larkin's *Collected Poems* to her study, but she wasn't in the mood for it tonight. She was considering teaching Larkin next term, in her graduate class; it would do her students good to read the work of a poet who wrote with great emotion yet without sentimentality or self-pity. She herself had always admired Larkin, although less for the poems than for the life he'd lived. She liked the work well enough (how could one *not* like, in particular, his most famous poem, "This Be the Verse"—*They fuck you up, your mum and dad*—the one poem of his that Larkin himself had eventually come to wish he'd never written?), but she didn't love any of it: it was too blunt and bitter for her. But the life! He had lived so uneventfully, had been so solitary. An antisocial librarian who'd never married. They might have been friends, she'd sometimes thought—if he'd had friends at all.

She heard Phil's nails clicking on the stairs and glanced up from *The Mercy* and her wineglass: he came in and shook his head, stretched—he was getting very long, she noticed; in just the two and a half weeks he'd been with her he'd grown considerably, which made her think he might turn out to be a big dog after all—and lay down with a groan at her feet.

"Soon, boy," she said. "Let me just check my e-mail"—she looked at her watch—"and we'll be on our way in half an hour."

He sighed and she bent down to rub his head. "My friend," she whispered.

He half lifted his head, looking quizzical.

"You're the only dog I've got, Phil." He gave her a piercing, surprisingly sober look. "That's right," she said, delighted.

He wagged his tail, but slowly, so that it struck the wood floor in a dignified way—a slow, steady drumbeat. *Thump. Thump. Thump.* "It's just you and me, babe," she told him as she stroked his head. "Very Sonny and Cher, don't you think?" She sang, softly, "*They say we're young and we don't know / We won't find out unti-i-ill we grow.*"

Phil grunted and she laughed. "I Got You, Babe" had been her favorite song the summer she was seven years old—an arcane fact of which she was aware not only because her mother enjoyed speaking of it (particularly in the company of her disco-dancing/yoga/condo buddies when Jill visited her in West Palm), taking pains to point out that it had been *both* Jill's and her own favorite song in the summer of '65 (that they had been like *this* back then), but also because a sheet of lined paper on which Jill herself had painstakingly printed the lyrics after listening to the song on the radio several hundred times still existed, signed (*Jill Rosen*—an artifact!—with a little flower for the dot over the *i*) and dated at the bottom of the page.

And she was in possession of this artifact. Her mother had passed it on to her when she moved to Florida, in a box in which there were also some of her earliest efforts at poetry (not as unlike "I Got You, Babe" as she might have wished, though the vocabulary and syntax were somewhat more advanced than *I got you to walk with me / I got you to talk with me*), a play she'd written in fifth grade, and several junior high school short stories. Why her mother had saved the song lyrics along with her literary juvenilia, Jill couldn't say. Nor why *she* kept them, still, in her study closet along with the rest of the contents of that box and the boxful of early writing *she* had saved—the published poems in her grade school, junior high, and high school yearbooks, and a stack of copies of *The Current,* her high school paper, from the year she'd had a poem on the back page of every issue.

Nor could she say, for that matter, what those lyrics could have meant to her, back then. Whom she could have been thinking of. An imaginary "you"? Presumably. A fictional, unknown, idealized, future you. The idea of *you.*

SHE WOKE UP the next morning to the surprise of snow. Phil's first snow! she thought when she opened the back door, then remembered that Phil would have known snow when he was still a stray, and she glanced down at him as they went down the steps that led into the yard, wondering if the snow brought back bad memories. Apparently not. He began at once to leap into the air, as joyful as she'd ever seen him, and when he landed after each leap he dug his nose into the snow around him and came up sputtering, shaking his head and flinging snow everywhere, then—not satisfied with the blizzard his head had caused—using his back legs to kick up a great storm. She laughed and he threw himself down in the snow, flipped over on his back and waved his legs. He was in ecstasy; he had been waiting all his life for snow.

She stayed out with him longer than usual, wishing she had already fenced the yard in so that she could let him off his leash, which it was clear he badly wanted. But there was no guarantee that he wouldn't take off—that if she called him, he'd come to her. Just to prove he didn't have to, he might not.

As soon as the weather improved, she promised

herself, she'd have a fence put in for him. And next winter, and all the winters of his life, he could play in the snow until he wore himself out.

It was not a teaching day, and she took her carafe of coffee up to her study, settled in for a morning of work. She'd been at it for a couple of hours when the phone rang, and when she got up to answer it—the only phone upstairs was in the bedroom—Phil came up the stairs to find out who it was. When she picked up the receiver, he jumped onto the bed to watch her.

"Is Jill there?" A male voice, unfamiliar.

"This is she." She patted Phil's head and he gave her what she thought of as his I-can-tolerate-this look—his head tilted and his eyes half closed—which made her grin.

"Jill, this is Bill. You know, the guy you got the dog from?"

"Of course, Bill."

She must have sounded taken aback, because he said, quickly, "I'm sorry to be bothering you. I didn't think I'd even catch you, tell you the truth, I figured I'd just leave a message. On your machine, you know? You'd be at work, so I'd—"

"I don't have a machine," she said—and then she felt uneasy; she hadn't meant to sound so...so prissy. Phil was watching her from the bed. "Actually, I'm working at home today. What can I do for you?"

"Really, no answering machine?" He made a sound that she thought must be what was meant by the word "chuckle," a sound she wasn't sure she'd ever heard before. "Man, you must be the only person left in the world without an answering machine!"

"I somehow doubt it," she said. "What can I do for you?"

Phil was watching her in a way she wasn't crazy about. A warning way. As if he were telling her: *Be kind. This man saved my life.*

"So what's up, Bill?" she said, before Bill had a chance to answer. She could be nicer; she could.

"I just wanted to see how you and Dog were getting on. I figured I'd leave a message letting you know that if you had any problems, you could give me a call. Lots of times after people take one of my fosters they call me up, just to let me know how it's going. Since I didn't hear anything...."

My God, she thought. Where was Miss Manners when you needed her? "I had no idea," she said. "I should have called."

"No, no, I don't mean you *should've*. No, nothing like that. I just meant...I just wanted to ask how it was going, that's all. Make sure everything worked out okay."

"It's worked out just fine," she told him. "Very well. Thank you."

"Well, that's good."

"Bill, it was awfully thoughtful of you to call," she said. "We're doing fine. Marvelously. I'm very grateful to you for bringing Phil into my life." Oh, no, that sounded dreadful—sounded like a cross between Lady Bountiful and a Whitney Houston song. What was wrong with her? Why couldn't she find the right note to strike? "So if that's all—"

"Well, and I wanted to say, you know, if it doesn't work out for any reason, if you'd let me know—I mean, if you'd let me have the dog back instead of just, say, taking him to a shelter or giving him away to somebody you know, or advertising—"

"I won't be giving the dog up," she said, more sharply than she should have. She looked over at Phil, who was looking sadder than usual. *All right*, she told him telepathically, *all right. I'll be nice. He means well, I'm sure.*

She kept her eye on Phil as she spoke. "It's good of you to make that offer, Bill. I can't imagine I'll need to take you up on it, but I'll keep it in mind."

"You're busy, I'm sure. I figured you'd be at work now anyway, and I'd just leave, you know, a message. I'm at work myself, and I shouldn't stay on the phone for more than another minute. Shouldn't even have made the call, I guess. Personal calls are pretty much…you know, frowned upon here."

She had the definite sense that she was supposed to ask where "here" was, that he was trying to be friendly, that—oh, lord, it suddenly hit her, he was making a "personal" call, he *was* being friendly, he was…what to call it? Courting her? Making a move?

Her life *was* a situation comedy.

"Bill, I've got to go, I'm sorry—I hear someone—"

"Oh, sure, I understand. Like I said, I can't really talk now either. Maybe another time."

Another time. Phil was frowning at her, she was sure of it. She frowned back at him.

"Okay, well, then, thanks, Bill, and so long—nice of you to check in with us," and she hung up before she'd even finished the whole sentence.

To Phil, glowering at her, she said, "What do you expect me to do? Go out on a date with Mr. Shucks? For *you*? He kept you in a cage, for Christ's sake."

Phil jumped off the bed and walked with great dignity out of the room and down the hall. Jill watched him turn left, listened to him make his click-clack, jangling way downstairs, waited for the thump and whoosh that signaled that he'd jumped back into the bergère—*his* chair, and never mind that it had cost her seven hundred dollars to have the chair made, upholstered in the dark red silk she'd bought at a good fabric store, then sent FedEx to the manufacturer, paying extra for the right to supply her own fabric.

"Oh, so you're not too mad at me to snuggle up on a silk cushion I provide for you, huh?" she called downstairs to him as she went back to her study, to try to pick up the strand of unraveled thought.

Bill, calling her to be friendly.

She shook her head in wonder and returned to her desk, picked up her pen, sighed. She drew a line through the six words she'd spent two hours on. Start again. Nothing there worth saving.

Over the next few days she half expected to hear from Bill again, and she resolved that she would be prepared this time, would be cool but polite, not unpleasant—not at all, and why should she be? She had nothing against the man. He was a reminder that Phil had not been with her always, that he'd had another life, and worse, a hard one, before he had come to live with her—a reminder that she didn't know everything there was to know about her dog and never would—but it wasn't fair to hold that against *him*. He was harmless. And he had saved Phil's life, after all. She had no business feeling anything but grateful to him.

Still, when he didn't call again, it was a relief. She hoped she hadn't hurt his feelings. But surely if he thought about it—she had told him, because he had asked, the day she went to his house and left an hour later with Phil, that she was a college professor and a writer, a woman who wrote books of poetry; she was a woman who wore three-hundred-dollar shoes, who was a New Yorker, who barely knew how to drive (and was still rather proud of this), who had had her chairs custom-made and covered with silk, who didn't date—surely, surely he would realize it was an absurd proposition. Bill and her! Bill and Jill. She grimaced.

Phil would have to forgive her. He *would* forgive her, she knew that. If he had ever been angry in the first place. For as one day passed and then another, as the weekend came, he showed no signs of having ever been displeased with her. She was beginning to think she'd imagined it, and it occurred to her that she might very well have imagined that Bill was interested in her, too. He might have been doing exactly what he'd said, and only that: making sure the dog had worked out for her, making sure there were no problems. Perhaps he wanted to be certain that she wasn't thinking of giving him up; he might even have feared that she'd take him to the pound that had threatened to execute him. It was touching, really, that Bill cared so much for the dogs he "fostered," that he still felt bound to them and would sooner take them back into his care than see them given up to anyone or anyplace else. It was *nice* of him. He was a nice man. A nice man whose hobby was taking in abandoned dogs—why was that so much beneath her? Well, it wasn't *that* that was so much beneath her. Or—it was true, it was hard to imagine such a hobby. Taking in dogs, putting them in cages, releasing them to people you had to size up quickly, strangers coming to your house. And Bill living alone—he seemed to live alone—with his own dogs, which she hadn't even seen. She'd never left the garage; they'd transacted their business right there in front of the wall of cages. Kennels. Crates.

"You're a good man, Bill," she'd told him, and he had shrugged it off. She guessed he knew that. Or else he didn't know what she was talking about—he was just going about his business, being himself.

As he had been when he'd called her.

Perhaps she simply couldn't trust herself to understand anyone's motives anymore, couldn't read people, wasn't fit for ordinary human conversation; she'd fallen too far out of the habit. The only relationship she had that made any sense to her was with her dog.

And honestly it *was* as close to an ideal relationship as she had ever come. If this was pathetic, so be it. It didn't *feel* pathetic. As they came into the house after their midnight walk on Saturday and she unleashed and uncollared him—"Jewelry off! Now, isn't that a relief, sweetheart?"—she thought it felt anything *but* pathetic. It felt profound. It felt…lifesaving. What was pathetic about that?

She knew Phil loved her. He did not have to express it with grand gestures, with clichés. She appreciated the lack of the grand gesture, which she had learned to mistrust years ago. Not from Philip the first (oh, Christ, she thought: him again? She'd thought she'd put that thought to bed)—Philip the first had had no gestures. No, she'd learned not to equate the grand gesture with true feeling from another of her long-ago ex-lovers—one she'd been involved with after she'd returned to New York, after graduate school—an actor named David, who would show up at her door and drop to one knee, clasp both hands to his chest, declare that he'd been pining for her since the last time he had seen her, that the sight of her made him feel faint. And she'd *bought* that—she could hardly believe it now, but she had. Just as she'd bought it from Earl, another actor. She'd gone through an actor phase, just as she went through an artist phase during graduate school—better artists than fellow poets, she had told herself, no doubt thinking of Philip but not owning up to it; and later, after David, after Earl, after one more actor—Dan, who drove a cab to earn his living and finally gave up acting, resigned himself to driving a cab for good, last she'd heard—she went through a string of poets, and discovered that she had been right: they were worse than the artists.

Earl used to bring her flowers, which he couldn't afford, and little gifts designed to show how well he knew her—always slightly off the mark. Then it turned out that Earl had been sleeping with someone else all along—a ballet dancer. A ballet dancer! How could he stand himself? And this had been going on from the first week that Jill had started seeing him. Not quite as bad as David, then, who had started seeing someone else, she later heard, a few days before he told her that he thought they would be better off apart, and that it wasn't her, it was all him. *All him*—the phrase invoked to soothe her.

They'd all been like that. Single-minded in their dedication to all-himness. Whether they were committed to playing it cool, their cards close to their chests, or to making a display of their attachment, it came down to the same thing: it had almost nothing to do with her.

The dog's devotion, on the other hand, was to her. He was dedicated to her, in his straightforward way. It was unshowy, subtle, but it could be counted on. She didn't even have to think about it unless *she* chose to. There was no danger of the dog leaving her, betraying her, lying to her, changing his mind about her.

There was a danger, however—she told herself this dryly, getting ready for bed, Phil resting on the bathroom floor (he was a polite dog; he never jumped into her bed before she got in it first)—there was a danger of her sounding like one of the students in her introductory undergraduate workshops, writing a love poem. Since when did she think in these terms? Being lied to, betrayed, left?

Phil was a dog, for God's sake. Named for a stack of books, only accidentally or coincidentally given the name of a long-ago, practically forgotten ex, a failed poet, a guy who hadn't been great shakes as a human being either, had he? She could just as easily have named the dog Marco or Roy. Or David or Earl. Just as accidentally.

There were only so many names available to choose from. She could have named the dog Tom, Dick, or Harry. Or Carlo—after Emily Dickinson's dog, the one her father gave her so that she'd be forced to get out of the house, to take him for daily walks. That had only worked for a while, of course.

She could have named the dog Friday. As perhaps she should have.

Or Fido. Bill had a point.

Keep things in perspective, she advised herself, turning off the water. "Let's go, Phil. Time for bed."

He knew the word "bed"; it was a word he liked. He straightened up and followed her.

A dog was still a dog.

But it could not be forgotten—particularly not as she climbed into bed and he leapt up into it after her, and as she rolled onto her side, into sleeping position, and Phil moved into the space she made between her knees and abdomen—that this was a dog who had, just by his presence, cured her long-time insomnia. For with Phil beside her in the bed each night, she fell asleep at once. There was barely time to register that she had closed her eyes. She slept soundly for six hours—at which point Phil woke up, which was predictable. The book she'd read on housebreaking had warned her that six hours was as long as a puppy Phil's age could hold out—and his stirring would wake her (though he was polite about it; he didn't bark, not while it was still dark out, while he understood that it was not yet time to start the day: he sat up and waited, silently, for her to wake up on her own). She would throw off the covers and say, "All right, Phil, let's go," and they would go downstairs and she would shrug into her jacket and the Payless boots, put his "necklace" and leash back on him and take him out back for a moment, and then they would come back in, everything came off again, and they would go upstairs—she would stop in the bathroom herself while Phil waited for her in the hallway—and then it was back to bed, to sleep for two, sometimes even three hours more.

That she had no trouble going back to sleep,

when in the past if she'd waked in the night or early morning, that was it, she was up for good—that she now slept eight hours every night, despite the interruption of her sleep (and the blast of cold air, which should have made matters worse)—she owed to her dog, just as she owed him her ability to *go* to sleep at once, after years, decades, of "onset insomnia," of lying in her bed tremblingly wide awake no matter how exhausted.

This could not be kept in *perspective*. There was no perspective to be had on a dog who had cured her of something that had plagued her for so long.

Here come my night thoughts
On crutches,
Returning from studying the heavens.

There was no perspective to be had on a dog who had chased away her limping, broken, bitter night thoughts. Who stayed by her side all night long, guarding her from what Charles Simic called "The Something." Who was, she thought—let's face it—the truest friend she'd ever had. Who asked of her only what she was able to give, and was so grateful for it. Who had done more for her than any human being she could think of, offhand, ever in her life. In her almost forty-five years.

A prince among dogs, Phil was, she thought sleepily. A *king* among dogs. The dog, the dog, the dog—why even think this way? Why *not* the dog? She fell asleep, a curl around the dog, with these words on her lips. *Why not the dog, for God's sake?*

SHE HAD BEEN cynical; she had been rude to Bill on the phone. She was ashamed of herself.

But not enough to call him and apologize.

She thought about him, though. The more she thought about him, the more sure she was that he *was* good. You'd have to be, to take in puppies. Then again, what did she know about good men? She'd never met one. None of the men she'd dated had been good men. Not if good meant kind, charitable, generous, compassionate. Not if it meant thinking of others. Doing unto others as one would have them do unto you. As one would have all the world do.

The categorical imperative, March Harris might point out.

Her colleagues? No one who relied on irony to meet the world, who spoke with scare quotes implied around everything he said, could be called *good*. Her father? He had been too innocuous to be good. A man who never spoke at all could not be said to be *good*. He would have stepped between her and her mother in any one of a thousand battles—ten thousand battles—if he had been good. In any case, he was dead. What good was good if you were dead?

She wondered—she forced herself to wonder—if she'd feel differently about Bill if he were even the least bit good-looking, not paunchy and so tall he'd had to duck in the garage, with his baggy pants pulled up too high, gigantic feet in muddy shoes. If he had been handsome like Philip the first, like David, like Earl (oh, Earl was the handsomest; she'd had a weakness, a terrible weakness, for a handsome man), like the other actor, the cab driver, Dan—would she have flirted with him?

No, she truly didn't think so. She had given up on handsome years ago. Years and years ago, long before she'd given up on men. She'd dated homely men—downright ugly men. But they were brilliant, or she'd thought they were. Bill was neither handsome nor brilliant. He was...only good.

And so she had thanked him, had taken the dog and written the check to cover the expenses he had incurred taking care of him, had accepted his list of instructions—hints, he called them—and ignored his advice about starting out a little "disengaged" and turning her back on the dog if he did something he shouldn't do. "Such as?" she asked. "Well, such as bite you," Bill said, and she said, shocked, "He's going to bite me?" Bill grinned. "He's still teething. He won't mean to hurt you, but he shouldn't be allowed to chew on you. So what you do is, you turn your back, you walk away, and you give him something acceptable to chew on, a toy or a stick of rawhide." But she didn't "disengage" at all, not for one second, and when the dog chewed on her fingers that first afternoon as they lay in the bed, collapsed together, she giggled and let him. She could not remember the last time she had felt this way.

She'd thought about goodness then, that first afternoon and night. That night as she lay awake, the dog in bed with her, her arms wrapped around him, she wondered if the pleasure it gave her to have the dog here with her meant that *her* taking in the dog wasn't good in anything like the way Bill's taking in dogs was. Well, of course it wasn't. He took them in to save their lives. But then he caged them. She could not get past this. That she had read the chapter about "crate training" in her trusty dog book, that many of the neighborhood dog-walkers, in those early days when she had walked among them, had told her they swore by it, hadn't helped; didn't help. If she allowed herself to think of it, of Phil locked up, Phil behind bars, tears sprung to her eyes; her heart constricted.

But perhaps Bill's caging the dogs he rescued was equal—if there were a formula, with points given for goodness, and points to be taken away—to her pleasure in Phil's company. Good to take the dog, less good to cage or to enjoy him.

And what of the motives that underlay Bill's taking in of the dog, of all the dogs (the dogs he saved and then imprisoned!) in the first place? She knew nothing about Bill's motives—pure goodness, was that a motive? And did it count as "good" that *she* had taken in the dog on impulse, without a plan? Not that her motives had been bad; she hadn't had any. She hadn't known what she was doing.

But perhaps that didn't matter, she thought now. It was not a question of whether she had taken the dog in for her sake or for his—it was that she'd done it for no sake at all. She had just *done* it. She hadn't fussed and planned—she hadn't thought. For once in her life, she hadn't *thought*! She had simply done what was right.

And that was goodness, wasn't it? Even if—perhaps especially if—she had done right by accident.

WORKSHOP, Monday morning. Thirteen boys and

girls around the table, frowning at the pages in their hands, arguing about the lineation of a long narrative poem one of the most ambitious among them had turned in. A girl—a young woman—named Charlotte. Who named a daughter Charlotte anymore? Jill asked herself idly, listening to them. She might, she supposed; she wondered fleetingly if Charlotte's mother were a poet. Or simply literary. A reader—rare enough these days.

Jennifer—"but call me Jenny, everybody does" (Jill didn't)—was saying that the line breaks in the second and third stanzas seemed almost random and didn't do justice to the poem. She kept glancing at Jill as she spoke, for confirmation. Jill was careful not to signal one way or another.

"Capricious lineation," Dylan said, and Jill kept her straight face. He was parroting her, yes, but she was pretty sure he wasn't aware of it.

She would never have named a child, male or female, Dylan. At least she didn't think so. And yet, over the years, she'd had *four* Dylans—two male, like this one, and two female. Was it possible that four mothers in this one Midwestern state had gone into labor without having settled on a name, and happened to have Dylan on the turntable? She could imagine something like this happening to her. Or, worse yet, Dylan and...Aretha, say, stacked and set to go. It happened often enough, in the evening while she was making dinner, drinking her first glass of wine. She might have ended up with Dylan Aretha Rosen. Or Aretha Dylan, which scanned better. Or how about Al (Green) James (Brown) Rosen? Al James, James Al. The second, definitely. But if she were pregnant, she wouldn't be drinking wine. She would be less likely to give in to a foolish, passing impulse. And imagine being pregnant for nine months and not having a name prepared! Unless one were pregnant and didn't know it. Wasn't this something that happened sometimes? She vaguely remembered reading something about such a woman. A teenager, though. Not a grownup, a middle-aged woman. A woman who in fact was unlikely to be able to get pregnant at all. It was too late, too late.

She'd lost track of the class. She must have done

something to let them know it, too—to let them know something—because they'd all stopped talking. Thirteen pairs of eyes were on her. The group operated like an auctioneer, she thought—they all did, all her workshops. Even the introductory classes shifted gears halfway through the term and learned to work together, all of them as one, their teacher on the other side, not necessarily the enemy but always the Other, the one whose opinion mattered most, who could with a word or even a look close down discussion. They watched her for the smallest sign—a half nod, a raised eyebrow—and missed nothing.

She smiled at them (and read *their* signs as well, saw them relax just slightly, waiting for her next move). "Let's talk about the voice, shall we? Especially as it begins to change in"—she glanced down at her notes—"the fourth strophe. Top of the second page. And then shifts again in the seventh strophe, on—"

"Professor Rosen?" This was Michael—pale, thin-faced, close-cropped white-blond hair, wire-rimmed eyeglasses, a gold earring and a silver bead on his left nostril. "Is the voice a function of the—"

"The voice is responsible for the tension between the lyric and the...the drama in it, I think." Jason, interrupting. A fat, sweating boy, dressed always in the University's logo-bearing caps and sweatshirts. A fraternity boy, she guessed. But he wrote beautifully. "Isn't it?" he demanded, looking toward Jill and then back to Michael.

"By 'drama' I assume you mean the narrative itself, right? Because there's no drama per se—no suspense, right?" Polly. Dyed black hair. Nose ring *and* eyebrow ring. Both silver. Even in February a strip of skin showed between miniature T-shirt and black jeans. "I mean, it's a story but it's not a story."

"Like a Henry James novel," said Jason. About half of them laughed.

"The voice isn't responsible for—"

"The drama is just—"

They were off and running, without her. She smiled, but secretly, holding the poem up to her face.

"I wouldn't even call this a lyric poem, not

when it's so—"

They might all have been her children, she thought.

Dylan said, "Do we need to review our definition of lyric poetry? This is pure emotion. The narrative doesn't undermine that. The voice—Professor Rosen wanted us to look at the voice, remember?—is so hushed and...oh, I don't know, gorgeous. Telling this story. With so much passion, but as if it's a secret."

"Not just as if it's a secret," Heather said. "As if he or she—the speaker in the poem—is a secret. As if he doesn't want us to know who he is."

"As if he's *nothing*."

"And he 'beholds the nothing that is not there and the nothing that is,'" Jason said. Triumphantly.

Her children gathered all around her at the dinner table. Another situation for the situation comedy. Her thirteen children.

Feasting on poetry, she thought, and snorted. They went silent instantly.

"No, no, it's fine, go on," she told them. But they

were all quiet now, watching her and waiting. She looked around the table at them. Dylan, and Michael—then Shari (terrible name!) on his left, then Kate ("no, never Katherine"), Charlotte, Jason, Polly, Jennifer, Matthew, Heather, Nicole, Emily, and Timothy. The last three were also in her afternoon class; they had "bonded," they'd told her. They always sat together now. Emily, talented but lazy. Nicole, oversensitive to criticism. Timothy, who could write a stunning line but not sustain it, and who was a football player, second string. His parents could not understand why he was taking poetry classes. Same with Matthew, who was slated for med school and was very bright and possibly quite gifted, but careless.

They really might have been her children.

They all looked so *expectant.*

"Honestly," she said to the class, "you're doing beautifully. It's a wonderful poem and you're all helping Charlotte make it better still."

Charlotte blushed; her eyes glittered. How often did Professor Rosen use the word "wonderful"?

How often did she say "better still"?

They all looked rather stunned. "Beautifully"? Had she said "beautifully"?

She bowed her head. She had no desire for them to see her own eyes glittering.

Not a situation comedy, she thought. Her *life*.

MIDNIGHT AGAIN. Cold again. A little drunk again. Not *that* drunk; drunk for her, that was all—too drunk to be running behind a dog on icy sidewalks. All the snow had melted after several days, but before evaporating, it had frozen hard. Now, walking in her Payless boots behind the racing dog was like ice-skating, which she had never in her life done and could not imagine anyone doing for pleasure. If she tried to stick to places that had been salted, the salt burned the soft parts of Phil's paws: he would sit down, whimpering, holding up first one paw and then another for her to pity.

So she slipped and slid behind the dog. She wasn't sure that being perfectly sober would make any difference. She simply wasn't athletic, had no natural grace or balance. No *physical* grace or balance. Mentally—well, mentally she prided herself on being extremely graceful (she might go so far as to call her mental bearing *elegant*) and she had been standing on intellectual, artistic tiptoes (on one foot—she amused herself, picturing this—with one leg in the air at shoulder height) for practically her whole life. That she looked ridiculous running for a city bus—in the old days, when there was a city bus to ride, when she had lived in a real city—had never troubled her. That she could not throw a ball, she felt, was an asset, not a *flaw* in her. She could not recall now which boyfriend of her late teens or early twenties had insisted on teaching her to cast a softball at him in Central Park on a series of the worst dates she had ever had, then finally gave up, pronouncing her "hopeless," then breaking off their romance.

Walking a dog was perhaps the most physical thing she had done in years, other than sex. Not that she had indulged in the latter recently. She preferred not to think about how long it had been—it made her abstinence seem more unnatural than she felt it was. And it wasn't so much *abstinence*: she had not made a decision to give up sex, only the clamor of romance because it was exhausting her, doing her no good and too much harm—but she had not considered the consequences of this decision. Or else she had not taken herself seriously. *Give it up? Oh, sure, you've given it up! We'll see about that.*

She had seen about that.

She shivered. She was freezing. She'd managed to put on a hat, but she had once again forgotten gloves, hadn't paused for socks, and certainly she should have put sweatpants on over her leggings, a sweater over her T-shirt before she put on her jacket. She should not have had that second—it might have been a third—glass of Côtes du Rhône.

She was becoming her own mother, she thought—not *like* her own mother, but a mother to herself: *wear a hat, what do you mean no socks, and that's quite enough you've had to drink, young lady.*

Well, somebody had to look out for her, she

told herself wryly—wryly, not grimly. She hoped it was wryly.

For sex to be had with a man—for sex to be had at her age, she corrected herself—one had to have dealings with him. Some kind of dealings. At the very least a friendly understanding—although she'd never had that sort of sex (perhaps it was too purely physical, too much like throwing a softball or going for a run—a brisk, invigorating sort of thing to do, not her physical style at all). Either a friendly, healthy understanding between otherwise abstinent people—or else the sort of high drama and upheaval that she'd made a decision to leave behind for good.

In her youth she had sometimes had a sexual encounter that was of another kind—she wasn't certain what to call it. A coming-together of passions. She had been too young to understand it, had tried—and once or twice the man in question tried—to make a "relationship" of it, and these efforts always failed. She had not appreciated the force of simple sexual passion when it was still possible for her. She could not recall—she honestly could not recall!—the last time a man had looked her over the way she had once been looked at, the sort of look that led to bed. At least once, to bed.

It was not, she felt, that she was no longer attractive. She had never been a beauty, but she had the kind of looks that appealed to certain kinds of men, especially to certain kinds of men once they had talked to her. Even passion that came her way came in part—in large part, perhaps—because of her mind. She had always known that. What she hadn't given any thought to, she supposed, was that there was something about her other than her mind that had played its part, something that when coupled with her youth drew certain men to her. What was mysterious was that none of that had changed: she was still small, not even five foot two (of course she wore those heels that made her, if not tall, then *feel* tall, a feeling she liked very much), and round (not fat—she had never in her life weighed more than one hundred and twenty-seven pounds—but she had large breasts and a rounded belly and child-bearing hips and a well-padded bottom); she still wore her hair long, and loose (despite her mother's harping).

She was still *herself*. Outside as well as in. But every part of her—even the breasts every man with whom she'd been involved had been more enamored of than she might have preferred (but they were so much softer and fell so much lower now); even the thick mane of hair on which men had been commenting since she was in her teens—particularly during periods when short hair was so fashionable she was likely to be one of the few women or girls in a given room who had long hair, and the only one whose hair was waist-length (but it was dryer and coarser than it had been in her youth, and it was graying now); even her still soft (she checked it daily) skin, sagging now around her jaw line (and on the back of her hand, if she pinched it, the skin stayed pinched long after she had let it go)—every part of her had *aged*.

You wouldn't think that this alone would make her so much less desirable.

And it had happened so suddenly! One day she was young, it seemed to her, and the next day she wasn't. Oh, but really she knew that this wasn't true—knew that middle age had crept up on her slowly, as it must for everyone (and indeed she had been watching time creep up on everyone around her, all the people with whom she'd been teaching for the last ten years, many of whom had been young, like her, when she had first arrived)—but still she *felt* ambushed.

Some time after she had taken this job, bought this house, begun saying no when men—not that there had been so many—asked her out to dinner, things had changed. *She* had changed. When she'd first started saying no to invitations, she had been exhilarated: why *not* say no? she'd asked herself, each time. It seemed that this had never crossed her mind before. *What do you have to lose?* was what she used to ask herself. And her answer had been, always, *Not much. What's a few hours? Get to know him. Who can tell what might come of it?* But she knew exactly what might "come of it," and now she looked around and thought there wasn't anyone she wanted, after all, to get to know. She remembered all too well the misery to which the getting-to-know led.

And yet—and yet—it hadn't crossed her mind that they'd stop asking. That they would stop *looking*. That they would stop picking up a lock of her hair and remarking—as if casually, her hair held loosely in their hands—"This is amazing hair. How long have you been growing it?"

She had never liked being appraised. How could she even think of missing it?

Perhaps she was only missing it tonight because she was a bit drunk. A bit—not very much; not more than usual. But she paused, startled, to consider this. *No more than usual.* Two glasses of wine's worth—perhaps three. No more, or hardly more, than that. The usual amount of wine; the usual amount of drunk.

She might, she told herself, when she was not the least bit drunk—in daylight, in one of those purely sober daytime hours of which there were so many—tomorrow, or the next day (*soon*, at any rate), sit down and think about her drinking habits, and decide if she might be in anything like trouble. Not much trouble—just some little bit of trouble.

But really, she thought, two glasses of wine! What were two glasses of wine? She had never had a problem with alcohol.

Never had a problem with alcohol, never intended to give up sex. Never even considered that she would ever own a dog. She thought of this now, thought of each of these things, quite seriously, as if the three were related. Were they related?

The relationship would be...what? Things she had done by accident? Fallen into the habit of drinking wine each evening—perhaps half a bottle one night, the other half the next? To unwind, after the day. For the sensuous pleasure of the wine—the taste of it, the smell, the way it made her feel. All of these. She hadn't that many such pleasures. But she hadn't meant to make a *habit* of it. Nor had she decided to make a habit of sleeping alone. Except now she didn't sleep alone: her dog slept in her bed with her. Two accidents, perhaps related.

Oh, but there were others. One could say it was entirely accidental that she lived in this town, a town she had not chosen, had moved to for a teaching job; and now it had become her home. She had lived here for ten years and would most likely never leave. Leave to go where? Back to New York? She had nothing in New York. She wouldn't know how to live, anymore, in New York.

And so she'd made herself an accidental home, an accidental life.

Even the teaching job, which had brought her to this city, could be said to be an accident. It was an accidental occupation. She had never set out to teach, never meant to be a teacher. She wrote poems, and then she had set out to earn a living. She had backed into her whole life, so to speak.

She was in danger, she noted, of feeling sorry for herself. At this thought, *sorry for herself*, she tossed her head—tossed her long, long hair, hair that according to her mother was not merely unbecoming but was *inappropriate* for a woman her age, not to mention (but of course her mother mentioned anyway) how much gray had turned up in it and that she *refused to do anything about it.* Her mother mentioned this, all of it, not *to* Jill but about her, in her presence, every single time she visited, to one or another of the other residents of her condo complex. They would nod in sympathy. They understood how it was: they all had children too who refused to do anything about anything.

She tossed her hair where it emerged below her knit hat that did very little to keep out the cold (her teeth were chattering by now, and she wondered, really, what *had* she been thinking, what was she thinking night after night, taking a dog out at midnight in mid-February in the Midwest without proper clothes? and resolved to outfit herself appropriately from now on, to act like the Midwesterner she had become)—tossed her one-third gray and two-thirds still, thank goodness, glossy-black, thick, heavy, waist-long hair of which she was still vain (the third of her three vanities: house, shoes, hair)—tossed her hair and asked herself: *With whom would you change places?*

It was her customary bracing question when she caught herself at the lip of the cavern of self-pity.

With whom?

If she caught herself in time, she would not lose her balance and pitch forward, down, down, into it. Not that she would not be able to claw her way out. But she could make better use of her strength; much better to keep upright, out of it altogether.

With whom?

Not any of her colleagues at the university—not one, female or male. (This one was easy, perhaps even too easy; by itself, it didn't help.)

A rival? She lined them up in her mind (she did not have to think very hard about this, for she knew exactly who they were: other female poets of her own age, with gifts roughly equal to her own but upon whom considerably more worldly success had been heaped) and ticked through their life-troubles: this one on her fourth unhappy marriage; this one extraordinarily homely, with poor skin and chronically sore feet of which she was forever complaining, removing her orthopedic shoes in public and rubbing her toes, never mind that others at the table with her might be eating dinner, others at the party in her honor drinking wine and nibbling on cheese cubes and crackers—a woman of whom it was often said, "Thank God she's brilliant"; this one an ex-junkie (which was no secret; she hardly ever wrote about anything else, and she'd gone ahead and *called* her most recent book *Ex-Junkie;* the one before that had been called *Junk*), brilliant enough too but crazy, terrified of people, so that she shrank back if anyone so much as spoke directly to her, and famous for politely excusing herself to throw up after the meals she was fed by the poets at the universities hosting her readings (and who had once told Jill, when she was visiting *this* university at Jill's invitation, and Jill suggested they stop in the airport bar for a drink while waiting for her flight out, "I'm sorry, I don't do that sort of thing. I'm not interested in friendships with other poets, only with people who can teach me something"). Then there was the daughter of a very famous long-dead poet who had fathered her in his late middle age and famously neglected her *and* cheated on her mother with both women and men, even in his late eighties, and who had left his diaries in the care of his literary agent to be published immediately after his death, so that reviews of her work always opened with a mention of her father's diaries.

There was the one who was Political and hadn't written a poem—or at least not published one—in seven years, so busy was she with her trips to Troubled Places in the Far Corners of the World. And then there was the one who had twice (twice that had been reported in the *Times*) tried to commit suicide, once in homage to Virginia Woolf (rocks in pockets in the Yaddo swimming pool, but it wasn't deep enough for her to drown in) and once in homage to Sylvia Plath (she even managed, though she was American, to find an oven in a London flat to put her head in while visiting an actress friend, who herself was famous enough for the attempt to have made *People* magazine).

How on earth might it be tempting to exchange lives with a single one of them?

Or with anyone she'd gone to school with—graduate school in Iowa, college in Manhattan, high school, junior high—she moved backwards through time quickly (she was experienced at this; she could check off every single person she'd once envied or simply admired—the younger, prettier girl poets who'd lived together in the house on Brown Street back in Iowa, whose careers had come to nothing, despite sleeping with the famous visitors who passed through the program; the other teaching-writing fellow with whom she had shared an office, who had published one good book the year after their graduation, then vanished forever; the two poets, boys, she'd known in college who had any talent, both of whom had gone to law school; high school friends who'd been both smart and beautiful—she could think of only two who fit that category, though there were five or six who'd been one or the other—who had married and had children young and come to nothing; self-possessed, glib junior high school classmates of whom she had been in awe before she knew any better) until she brought herself to age four and the brick semi-detached house in Flushing and her best friend, Naomi, who lived across the street, and no, she would not exchange lives with Naomi, either, no matter how Naomi's might have turned out. Even at four the beautiful Naomi, spoiled by her gentle, loving parents with too many toys and too much attention, was docile, passive, not the sort of person Jill even at four had any real desire to be. She had been able to bully Naomi into playing anything *she* wanted to play, and always with Naomi's toys. Such traits did not disappear as one grew older. Instead, Jill had observed, personalities would harden into place with age. Only when one was very old, it seemed to her—so old that everything that had hardened might dry and become brittle and at last break off—did one finally begin to change.

Her brother? She came last, as always, to her brother. Norman Stephen Rosen—five years her junior and already a full professor of linguistics.

(A nice sort of joke, she'd thought for years, on her tin-eared mother, that both of her children had grown up to be people who lived by the sounds of words.)

Of course, Norman taught at a university that was much less stringent than hers when it came to promotion. Not a state-supported university but one affiliated with a religion. Lutheran, she thought, or Catholic—she could never remember, which irritated Norman. He edited a journal too, one with a slightly less ridiculous name than hers: *Linguistics Q*. He was well-known in his field, a field in which, Jill reasoned, being "well-known" meant even less than it meant to be a well-known poet. Well-known by perhaps a hundred people. Unknown by the rest of the world.

At least if you were a published poet there was a slightly better chance of being known after your death.

Her brother had a wife, three children the wife looked after when she wasn't teaching part-time for very little money at Norman's university, and a sports car the wife and children could not fit into. He lived in a more interesting city and earned more money than Jill did—these were the chief reasons she envied him—and he had very nearly left his wife for one of his students last year. He had told his sister this in a series of e-mails she had not been able to keep up with, though she had tried at first. They came three, four times a day for weeks. After the first week she gave up, and he didn't even seem to notice: he just kept sending them, until he had exhausted himself, and the affair, apparently, had exhausted *it*self.

Norman Stephen Rosen went by N. Stephen Rosen; his wife and all his friends—and presumably the girl he'd nearly run off with, whom he had never spoken of again—all called him "En." Jill herself could not shake the old habit of calling him Norman. He called her nothing at all; she had noticed long ago that he simply avoided using her name. Even his e-mails opened without greetings: he came straight to the point—which, during those weeks last year, had been *I could not be more unhappy!* or *I tell you, it simply grows more insupportable each day*. He had always had a melodramatic, a self-dramatizing streak.

No, she would not change places with her little brother, either.

There, now, she thought. *That's better.*

BY THE END of the week the temperature had begun to rise, unseasonably. Crocus, planted by the former owners of the house, came up amid the English ivy and the periwinkle. Later there would be narcissus, iris, yarrow; the blowsy, hot pink peonies would bloom and droop, and ants would congregate on every fat pink flower. Everything that grew around the house had been put in by its former owners; all *she* knew about her garden was what all the plants were called—she'd looked them all up before the closing—and that if she did not hire a student to weed the front yard each summer, it became unmanageable and, after a while, quite ugly. She would have *asked* the sellers the names of the plants in the yard—she was eager, always, to have at hand the names of things—but she wasn't certain, then, how much one was supposed to simply *know*: if asking might strike them as every bit as strange, as hilarious, as not knowing the word for *grass* or *rose* or *pinecone.* In fact she wasn't certain still, after a decade, how much and what kinds of things were thought of here as common knowledge.

Now that spring was coming, she had bought herself a new dog-walking hat—a stocking cap, striped and tasseled, at Target (on clearance, one of the few winter items left)—and it had been days since she'd forgotten to put on her gloves before the walk. She was even wearing sweatpants over her leggings. And—she was perhaps most proud of herself for this—she'd remembered last night and tonight both to pause and put on socks before she dipped her feet into her dreadful boots.

She was stubborn, she knew. Stubborn as Phil. She had not wanted to make the adjustment to being a dog-walker, a Midwesterner. She was accustomed to working all year round in leggings and a T-shirt, barefoot—more stubbornness, in fact, for to do this in the wintertime she was obliged to keep her house profligately warm, re-creating the environment of the overheated New York apartment she had lived in for so many years. Well, she'd been *here* ten years now. She'd learned to drive a car, which she had not thought possible ten years ago. She'd bought her Payless boots and now a Target stocking cap. She was wearing socks and sweatpants! Perhaps it was time to complete the transition: lower the thermostat, dress warmly while at home. Her frugality, which was extensive and for which she blamed her mother—she had learned it at her knee!—had certain limits (chief among them heat, good furniture, and shoes), but she never *spent* without a flush of shame. There was a battle in her, always, she thought, between her resistance to her Middle Western life and what she saw as its petty economies and lack of elegance—its utter stylelessness, its pragmatism—and her own tendency toward parsimony (which, she had to concede, had been helpful through the years in New York when she'd had to stretch the meager and sporadic income of a freelancer to make ends meet). Sometimes it seemed to her she was extravagant simply to prove to herself that she *could* be, even here. The ugly, cheap boots—she glanced down at them and frowned—had been a concession, not only to *here*, and to dog-walking, but to her own nature.

Soon she wouldn't need to wear these boots; she'd have to buy a pair of clogs or slip-on sneakers at Payless or Target. Oh, she was crossing hurdles left and right now, wasn't she? Think of all the years she had flat-out refused to be a Midwesterner—reading the *Times* instead of the appalling local paper (the name of it alone was irritating to her: *The Herald-Tidings-Messenger,* the result of a three-way merger forced by the *Herald* family publishing dynasty, the Foxes—"the illiterate man's Sulzbergers," Jill called them, a joke that only a handful of her colleagues seemed to get—after having crushed the other two, marginally better papers by refusing them the use of the printing plant the Foxes owned) and doing her shopping on one coast or the other, or in a pinch in Chicago—"the damned-by-faint-praise best of the Midwest," she called that city—when she traveled for a reading or a conference. And on those travels, when she was asked where she was from, always saying "New York City. Flushing, Queens, originally. Then Manhattan, in the Village. But I live now in ____________," and she would at last, reluctantly, name the town in which she'd lived for so long, in which she owned a house, in which she had a job from which she could not be fired—even if she would not be promoted. In which, now, she had a dog. For whom she would have to make arrangements when she traveled, she now realized. It would be the first time in her life she'd have to make special arrangements when she traveled, the first time she'd have to do anything more taxing than dropping off a hold-mail card at the post office and calling the *Times* to have them stop delivery, which was spotty anyway. *The New York Sometimes,* she would tell her students it was called here. Some of them would laugh.

Who would take care of Phil the next time she left town? A student? One of the students who had laughed when she announced that she now had a dog? But perhaps the vet could help with this. Or perhaps she'd stop traveling anywhere for a while. Or perhaps, she told herself, she'd stop fooling herself: the invitations to give readings or appear at conferences were fewer each year. She had made no trips at all last year except for a short, miserable visit with her mother in mid-April and to the MLA conference in December—and she had gone to MLA only because the conference, for a change, had been held in New York, giving her a chance to go home (so she still called it, still thought of it) on her department's dime. The truth was, until the publication of her third book, the book she hadn't finished writing—wasn't anywhere near finished writing—she wasn't likely to be going anywhere. She could stay home with Phil to her heart's content.

Home. Was *this* home, then?

And was this—home, with her dog—what would make her heart content?

"Phil, for God's sake!"

The dog had stopped to sniff around a tree, and she had to stop short behind him, so abruptly she almost ran into the tree herself. "Come on, Phil, a little consideration!" He didn't look up; he was busy with his tree (what kind of tree? It struck her that she ought to know. She would make it her business to look up the names of all the trees around the neighborhood).

Phil was digging in the newly softened dirt that had unfrozen near the tree, sticking his nose into the hole he'd dug and emitting snuffling noises that made her smile. She didn't mind taking a short break. They'd been out for three-quarters of an hour and he had run her hard tonight. So even though she wasn't cold—she wasn't a bit cold! she marveled—she was tired. After this adventure with the tree, she was ready to get the dog home. In fact she had been gently nudging him in that direction for the last fifteen minutes, without even having to think about it. She'd learned to do that—to discreetly maneuver him toward home after half an hour, slowly, so he wouldn't notice she was doing it, if she hoped to finish up the walk within the next half hour.

After a few minutes of his poking and sniffing

and snuffling, she tugged on the leash, not too hard, just enough to let him know she was still there. He ignored her. Well, it wouldn't kill her to wait another minute. *Where's the fire?* she asked herself, and that drew her up short, for it was an old private joke, a joke between her and Philip, Philip the first, of all people. "Where's the Fire?" had been the title of a poem of his that he had written in response to one of hers—"Fire Escape," which would later be the title poem of her first collection. But that was long after Philip. When she showed the poem to him—she had shown him everything she wrote, as soon as she felt it was finished—he told her he found it a bit "solemn." Then a few days later he turned up at her place with a poem of his own: a jokey, teasing poem that had been genuinely funny, she recalled. It made her laugh and defused his criticism. And afterwards, whenever one of them felt that the other was being too serious about something that wasn't worthy of such gravity, he or she would interrupt with, "Where's the fire?"

Phil was still nosing around the tree.

It was mostly habit, she knew, that made her impatient with him. She simply wasn't used to waiting for anybody else. But really, what was the big rush? Neither she nor Phil was wanted anywhere. What was five minutes, this way or the other?

So she tried to wait patiently. It wasn't that she wasn't capable of patience. Writing poetry had taught her patience. Teaching, she had found that all this patience came in handy. But she'd had no idea how patient she would have to be sometimes, just walking a dog. The kind of patient she had never been with any human being.

"Phil," she said—not sharply; nicely—"it would be good to go to bed sometime in the near future, wouldn't it?" She could be patient with him, but *he* could learn to be a little more responsive. If she could learn to drive a car, buy a stocking cap at Target, wear cheap man-made boots—even consider taking the thermostat down a few notches from 75°—couldn't he give an inch or two?

But she didn't think he could. She watched him, so intent on his "work"—his doggy work. That was what mattered to Phil—not that she was waiting, tired, ready to go home. She didn't doubt his love, but it was love up to a point. If he could talk to her, he'd say, *Oh, for the love of God, woman! The ground has just begun to thaw!! Do you know what kind of delicious, fascinating, not to say* astounding *smells are rising from it? No, you don't, do you, now! You can't even imagine. My God—what's that smell? And that? Good smell! Glorious smell! Oh, no—no, no, no*—terrible *smell. Scary smell. Ah, now that's better. Interesting....*

His own dog, going about his life's work. His work, his hobby, and his habit all rolled up in one. *This is what matters to me. Leave me to it in peace, for pity's sake.*

He reminded her, a little bit, she realized then, not only of Philip but of all of them, every man she'd ever known. Even her brother. Even her mute, gentle father. *He* had gone about his business without letting anything get in the way of it. He left for work each morning and returned each evening smelling of the cold, the subway, the city itself. Her mother reporting with an air of grievance whatever had transpired. His silence, in response. And then the *Post* had to be read, the TV news solemnly watched. He might go all day, days on end, without saying anything to them—to her mother, to her brother, to her—except "Good morning," and "Good evening," and then finally "Good night." None of them knew what went on in his mind, what world he was living in. Only that it wasn't theirs.

Her brother, leaving home at seventeen for college in California, on scholarships that meant their mother couldn't hold him back, as she'd been trying to do since he'd started filing applications. "Queens College is free! Abso-*lute*-ly free! This is a deal you're going to get somewhere else? Foolish people think they need to pay through the nose for something to be worth anything, but it's not true. What's free is as good as what costs. Sometimes what's free is *better* than what costs." Norman even had a job lined up at school, way in advance, so that he didn't need to ask for anything—he just left, oblivious to all the hand-wringing and histrionics.

Or maybe not oblivious. Maybe just focused, undistractible. And really there had been a lot less to distract him. Their mother had never badgered him, the way she'd badgered Jill, about his choice of major or his occupation. That Jill had "ended up a teacher after all" was a source of great amusement to her mother, who liked to crow that she had always known this was what Jill should do—that her daughter could have saved herself a lot of time and trouble if she'd only studied education in the first place, "like I told her to," and gotten a job in the New York City public school system.

Norman had done exactly what he wanted to do, had gone about it with a sense of self-importance that was casual, reflexive. He was dogged in his pursuit of what interested *him*. His mother, his sister, his wife, even his children—even his young girlfriend—hadn't gotten in his way, gotten under his skin.

That was all *she'd* ever wanted. To be able to go about her business undistracted. Like a man. Like every man she'd ever dated, slept with, broken up with, given up on, put behind her. Put behind her for good.

Yet here she was, waiting patiently for Phil. She yanked on his leash. "Let's *go*. I'm tired. I want to go home."

Which was not the way to get him to go home. She knew that. They were on their way there now—only two blocks away! Two blocks that were taking them twenty minutes or more to traverse. Had she not begun, half an hour into their walk, to delicately urge the dog in the direction of home? *Good boy, Phil. What a good boy you are! What do you suppose you'll find over* this *way, Phil?* If she had let the dog know, straight out, that she wanted to go home, if she had tried to *order* him—or, God forbid, pull him—in that direction, he would have stood his ground or tugged the other way. Which had been her experience, of course, with men. All those men going about *their* business, so undistractible, so *dogged*. If one wanted anything from any one of them, one couldn't ask, much less demand. One had to coax and nudge. It wasn't even *subtlety* that was required; it was deviousness. In fact, there was nothing subtle about the deviousness. It was painfully obvious, it seemed to her. *What a good boy you are!* indeed.

Feminine deviousness was what it was. And it had wearied her; the *what-a-good-boy* had worn her out. That, and the plain fact that nobody could ever be troubled to coo *What a good girl.*

And when it came to the dog—who true to form was refusing to budge, since she had given him a direct order—the fact that she didn't mind, that most of the time she even found his obstinacy entertaining, admirable, *lovable,* had to be because she did not expect him to be human. And that she found the necessity for clever manipulation on her part not enraging but amusing, must be, she supposed, because she could chalk her own behavior in this case up to *human* deviousness.

Still: "Enough is enough, Phil," she said now. Said it in a way that made it clear that she meant it this time. He looked up at her, surprised. "That's right, my friend."

She walked, he walked; they headed homeward.

WALKING THE DOG. It was all she ever did anymore.

Not *all.* She taught her classes, wearing her wool skirts, her silk blouses and her cashmere cardigans, her pearls. And she still wrote a poem once in a while, though not so often lately. When she *was* writing, it went slower and slower. One line one day; the second line a day or two later. Each line scrupulously made, so slowly she thought sometimes it was more like *un*writing, and how was she to finish the third book at this rate? The book that she was tentatively, not quite jokingly, calling *Breach of Promise.* She taught her classes and wrote a few words here and there and then unwrote them and wrote new ones and cooked dinners for herself and ate them by herself. Unless you counted the dog, eating his puppy kibble in the corner of the kitchen.

She taught and wrote and ate (exactly the same dinner two days in a row: cooked it one night, ate it two nights—the price of cooking for one) and read (though never in her bed at night—a thirty-five-year habit, broken) and took the dog out to the yard and *walked* the dog, night after night, and drank decent but not truly excellent wine—drank too much wine, she was almost certain now, thinking about giving it a rest for a week just to prove she could—although she told herself (told herself now, as she and Phil finished their walk, as they came up the front steps and she opened the door) that she shouldn't worry, really, she had never tended toward addiction, it was not her style—unless you counted men, "romance," love. There were books that counted love. Not the sort of books she'd ever read. But she'd seen them advertised, seen them in bookstores. Twelve-step plans to curing love addiction. No, not "curing." One was not cured: one was *in recovery*. She had gone out for six months when she was in her early thirties with a journalist who was a "recovering alcoholic"—*once addicted, always addicted,* he would tell her somberly, and *you can take the alcohol out but you can't take out the ism—*

and with a trumpet player (eight months, nearer to her middle thirties, one of her last "boyfriends" in New York) who spoke of himself as "a person in recovery." (How could she have brought herself to go to bed with men who used such phrases?) One was *never* recover*ed*, they had told her; one was always *in the process* of recovery.

The hell with that, she thought. She looked herself in the eye in the bathroom mirror. *She* was recovered. She'd given up love long ago.

Would giving up drinking be easier or harder?

She considered herself in the mirror. She looked tired, she thought.

Tired and old. She brushed her teeth with her eyes closed.

Stripped off her CCNY T-shirt, her gray sweatpants, her black leggings, her socks and her underwear, balled them up and sent them down the laundry chute.

She'd given up insomnia. She could give up drinking.

Day three without a glass of wine. She was nothing, she told herself, if not true to her word: if she said she was going to do something, she would do it—even if it were only to herself she'd said it—and she was proud of this, but she didn't suppose it counted as a vanity.

Day three of sobriety and she was doing fine.

There, she told herself. *I told you I didn't have a problem.*

And since she was doing fine, she thought, on day four, since she had proved that she could do very well without her evening glass or two of wine, there was no reason to go longer than the week she had decided it would take to clarify, solidify, make incontrovertible that proof. There was no point, after all, in getting carried away, in depriving herself of something she enjoyed just for the sake of deprivation. Plus, she wasn't falling asleep quite as quickly as she had been. To be sure, she was still going to sleep without the sleep-aid of a book, but it was taking longer, stone sober; she was spoiled, she guessed. She *liked* going to sleep as soon as she laid her head down. And when she woke with Phil in the middle of the night for his bathroom break and hers, the whole experience didn't have that somnolent quality she hadn't even known she enjoyed—floating downstairs in her nightgown, stepping out back into a pool of silence, to the yard that felt at that hour like another room of her house, a room in the world—and she missed it; it felt banal now, felt like nothing but being outside in the dark in a nightgown and jacket and the ugly clogs she'd bought at Target, a dog peeing sleepily while she yawned and tried not to fully awaken. With Phil curled up beside her in the bed afterward, she was still able to get back to sleep without much difficulty, but she was annoyed that she'd had to get up at all. She *was* spoiled now, she realized.

At the end of the week, to celebrate—although she wasn't sure whether she was celebrating her sobriety or its end—she sprang for a nineteen-dollar cabernet and two enormous artichokes *and* an eleven-dollar porterhouse at Giant Eagle (the steak would do for two nights, she was sure, and she steamed both artichokes tonight, for efficiency's sake). She drank three-quarters of the bottle while she cooked and ate her dinner. It took over an hour to eat, one artichoke leaf at a time, dipped in a delicious vinaigrette, which explained to some extent how she managed to drink quite so much. She drank a little more while cleaning up. Well, it was a celebration—a celebration of something or other—wasn't it?

And so she was drunker that night than she'd ever been while walking Phil. Drunk enough to lurch, to stumble twice, three times, behind him as he pulled. Once her left clog came off and she had to stop, yank hard on Phil, and go back to retrieve it, dragging him along.

He noticed the difference in her. All through their walk he kept stopping to look backwards, with an anxious expression that touched her, as it seemed to say, "My dear, are you sure you're quite all right?" No doubt his canine instincts would allow him to pick up on any changes in her, even subtle ones—he knew her so well by now—and there was nothing subtle in her staggering along on her end of the leash, particularly after a week of smooth sobriety. But what she wondered now was whether he knew what *caused* whatever changes he perceived in her—if he had observed, for example, that for a whole week she hadn't poured a glass of wine; if he had watched her drink nearly a whole bottle tonight. He must smell it on her, anyhow, she thought. Wouldn't a smart dog put it together—the scent or the lack of it, the changed gait? Who knew what else he was observing, sniffing out, interpreting, and cataloguing?

She tumbled into bed that night—a little dizzy, she realized only then—and Phil, leaping in just seconds behind her, put his front paws on her chest as she lay on her back contemplating the room spinning, trying to decide if she were going to be sick.

"I'm all right, Phil," she assured him. "Don't worry about me."

Her head had begun to ache, and the sensation of the room spinning around her was unpleasant, but not quite unbearable. Just short of unbearable. She was almost certain she was not going to be sick.

She would be all right—what she had told Phil would turn out to be true, even if it weren't true right at this minute—once she'd gotten a few hours of sleep.

She closed her eyes and Phil put his head down on his paws, on her chest. Protecting her. Protecting her, she thought as she tried by the force of her will to stop the bed from tilting, from herself.

Phil groaned, and if she hadn't known better, she would have told herself that he was protesting her thought. *That's the one thing I can't do,* she might have imagined that her dog was telling her.

But her dog was already asleep. He fell asleep faster than any creature she had ever known. Of course, the only creatures she had ever known before were men.

Phil groaned again. Dreaming, she supposed. He was no mind reader. He was a dog. Why did she have to remind herself of this so often?

She opened her eyes cautiously (actually, she found that it was better with her eyes open: the bed righted itself; the room's spin slowed) and by the dust of streetlight that snuck in all around the edges of her curtains, she watched Phil sleep. He trembled; he let out a quiet whimper. She whispered, "Shh, Phil, it's okay," and laid her hand on his head. He sighed.

Dreaming God knew what. Dog dreams.

She would like to know, in fact, she thought as she drifted toward sleep herself. A drunken sleep in which she might for once not dream at all. It was funny, really—this was her last thought before she slept—how *much* she would like to know.

SHE DID DREAM. She had a drunken dream in which, drunk, Bill came to her door, came pounding on her door and yelled at her to open it, and when she did, he told her he was taking Phil away. He didn't call him Phil, though—he called him Dog. And she said—she was drunk in the dream too, and she was trying to rise above her drunkenness, so that she sounded haughty—"Don't you call him *Dog*. His name is Phil, goddamn it, and he's *mine*." And Bill laughed at her and looked down at her. In the dream, at this point in the dream, he towered over her. In real life, it was true, he was tall and she was short—there might have been twelve, fourteen inches between them—but in the dream he was a giant; she was tiny. He looked way down at her and he didn't seem drunk anymore and he said, coldly, "Yours? *Your* dog? What are you talking about?"

She woke up in tears, and all day—thank goodness it was not a teaching day—she felt fragile and afraid. It didn't help that she was hung over. Her first hangover since graduate school—since her first *weeks* of graduate school, after which she'd stopped going out drinking after workshop. It seemed she had no ability to control her drinking, to control anything, after she had listened to poems—her own poems or anybody else's—being criticized. It was too much like watching an autopsy. It made her feel sick, and afterwards she'd drink to quell the sickness. Then the next day she would be hung over.

So she'd quit the weekly sessions at the bar. She could see even then that this distanced her from the others; even the teetotalers would go out with the group right after workshop, and drink ginger ale and talk until they were wound down enough to trudge back to their rooms—or pair off and wander home together, the pairs changing with a frequency that dizzied even her, with her long history of misbegotten romances. But it was worth it, opting out: she would go home and write, immediately, after workshop—writing in a fever that was fury mixed with desperation and determination (to *show* them! to get it *right*!). She wrote some of her best poems on Monday nights while all the other poets were out drinking.

But that was twenty years ago. She had long since ceased to write in desperation, in a fury; she had long since overcome her aversion to sitting in a room while criticism was dispensed. Well, she'd had to: she made her living at it. But truly she no longer thought of criticism as pathology, or even as surgery at all. It wasn't medicine she practiced in her classes —the poem spread before her for examination, diagnosis, a series of deft incisions (then, like magic, a cure—or else the pronouncement of incurability, at which all present would sigh and look solemn). It was not like that at all. No, what she was, she felt, was an archaeologist, leading a dig. It was exhilarating, an adventure. It did not—could not—make her ill. It made her feel smart and useful.

This was ironic, it occurred to her. Sitting in workshops as a student, she had felt stupid and useless. That was surely part of what had nauseated her and made her feel so faint.

She still didn't fare so well when others criticized *her* work. But she never had to endure that in public now, only in reviews or in rejection letters. And her reviews were generally good: people didn't usually bother to write bad reviews of poetry; they would simply not review the book at all if they didn't like it—a civility that was rare otherwise in life. Rejection letters were another matter. They would leave her feeling outraged if they were specific, pointed, detailed—and insulted if they were too vague, impersonal, and general. But they could be read in privacy. What she'd hated most in workshop when her poems were "up" was the public nature of the criticism. It was remarkable, really, that she had become a teacher, when she had so hated being taught.

She nursed her hangover, and by evening it was over with. But she still felt terrible—her eyes kept welling up, and she caught herself looking at Phil in a furtive, anxious way. Which of course *he* noticed. It made him tense and wary, and all day they circled each other—the dog whining, barking for no reason she could see, alternately staying close (too close; following on her heels as she went from room to room) and avoiding her, going so far as to get up and walk out of the room if she entered it. Two hours one way, two hours the other, unpredictably (he stayed away from her while she ate her leftover steak and picked at a few leaves of the artichoke), and by midnight, when she went looking for him for his walk, she was worn out, miserable.

The trouble was, the dream had started something. She didn't know exactly what it was until she was out walking with Phil, whom she had found at last in the basement, sleeping on top of a pile of dirty laundry under the chute's opening. She hadn't had anything to drink tonight—she wasn't crazy; she wasn't self-destructive (and just now it was hard to imagine ever wanting to drink anything again)—and she was impatient, edgy, sterner than she could remember ever before being with the dog while they took their walk. Several times, when he stopped to take a few minutes to sniff at something, she jerked the leash and said, "For the love of God, Phil, get moving. I don't have all night," and when he was pulling her along Angel Road, she pulled right back, let him cough and gag—and then, a moment later, consumed with remorse, ran up to him and bent down and put her arms around his neck, telling him that she was sorry, saying, "I'm just not feeling like myself tonight, I'm afraid. You can forgive me, can't you, boy?" But he wasn't having any of it; he turned his head away. *Too late,* he said. *You can't make it right.*

It hit her when the walk was almost over, as they were heading home, turning onto Vaida Avenue, where she had to watch her footing because there were hardly any squares of sidewalk that lined up properly, and to make matters worse, it was the darkest street in the neighborhood, so it was impossible to watch where you were going. Even sober, it was dangerous. Why had she let Phil take her this way? They could have gone the long way around and avoided this mess.

But they were halfway up the block now, and she had just tripped and nearly lost hold of the leash, and it hit her suddenly that Bill had called her not because he was interested in her *or* to kind-heartedly check up on the well-being of a dog he couldn't help caring about after saving his life and looking after him for weeks—or even as a courtesy, just to make sure Jill was a satisfied customer—but because he was afraid he'd made a mistake, because it had occurred to him that he should not have let her have the dog. That only a lapse in his ordinarily good judgment—because she was attractive; because she was intimidating—had led to his handing the dog over to her. What had he been thinking? That was what he wondered now. Certain signals he had missed when he had met her had come back to him.

She didn't know what those signals might have been—how could she know? She didn't know what made a good home for a dog, what sort of person had any right to have a dog like Phil live with her—but she could not imagine, now that she was thinking about it, that she hadn't done a damn good job of signaling her unsuitability, her downright unfitness. That Bill had missed the signals, she could chalk up to *how* intimidated he must have been. There she was: the college professor, the writer, the New Yorker in her black leather jacket and long hair and high-heeled Via Spiga boots. But then he'd thought about it, and while he wasn't a quick thinker—in fact, she could imagine that it took him quite a while to work things out, because obviously this guy was no genius, but she also felt sure that once he worked them out he would do a pretty good job of getting everything right—or someone who was able to take action quickly, or (unlike the Bill in her dream) a banger-on-doors, a bully, he had figured it out, figured *her* out, and now he was just trying to find a way to say what he wanted to say.

And he hadn't said it, that day when he had called her, because the right words hadn't come to him—the right words wouldn't come too easily to him, ever—or because he was too polite, or both. She intimidated people—men, especially—all the time, didn't she? Her mother had been telling her that for years.

So…now what? He didn't want to insult her—"I don't mean anything by this," he would say—but he had to tell her (he would say this gently) that it had become clear to him that he should never have let her take the dog.

She and Phil were halfway up the front steps to the house and she stopped, just stopped, one foot on the third step and one on the fourth. This was absurd—this was insane. *Her* dog. Bill had no right to judge her. He couldn't take the dog from her; he had no *rights* to the dog. He'd given up the dog.

She was shaking. She felt as if the phone call had already come, that she had just hung up the phone, enraged. She tried talking to herself: *this is crazy, nothing whatsoever has happened,* and *you don't even* know *that Bill is thinking along these lines.* But she was trembling as she got herself moving again, opened her front door, got inside and locked the door behind her. She unclasped Phil's collar—"Jewelry off," she forced herself to say, and, "Time for bed, boy"—but she had begun to cry, not just to cry but to sob, and it felt as if she had been waiting all day long for this, and then it seemed to her that it hadn't been just all *day* long but a long, long time, and she didn't even bother going to her chair, she just let herself go down on the floor right where she was, there by the door, and sobbed. And Phil, who had started up the stairs to the bedroom, turned and came back down—she heard him on the stairs, heading away and then heading back—and he came to her and sat down beside her. He pushed his nose through all her hair to get to her face, rubbed his muzzle against her cheek. *Don't cry. Don't cry.*

But she was lost—she cried and cried. She couldn't stop. Not for a long time. And all the while Phil sat beside her rubbing his head against hers, her hair falling around both of them like a curtain giving them some privacy together. *There, there. There, there.*

ALL RIGHT, she thought. All right. It wasn't so much that the dog had taken over her life—she told herself this, calmly, the day after what she referred to in her mind as the Episode—even if she'd had much of a life to be taken over; it was simply that he had taken over her *thoughts*. Which might as well, she recognized, be her life.

But why was this assumed to mean that she was without feelings? When the students in her prosody class had laughed at her for agreeing with them that she was not a "dog person," she had been hurt, and not because she wished to be the sort of person who was expected to own a dog (to *own* a dog! *Live with* was the phase she now preferred, when it seemed inappropriate to continue to speak of having "adopted" Phil, as if she were bragging about having taken him in, calling attention to the good heart she wasn't even sure she had) but because her students couldn't see (could anyone?) that it was possible to live with a dog, to love a dog and be loved in return, *without* being that sort of person. That it was indeed quite possible to be *the sort of person* that Professor Rosen, J. T. Rosen the poet, was, and have something else besides. A dog, for example. Love, perhaps.

After they had finished laughing at her that day, one of her students said, "You know, really, the thing is, you just seem too...I don't know...." *Dignified* was the word Jill thought she was searching for, but another of her students finished for the first one, "You don't seem as if you'd want to be bothered with something so...so concrete," he said, borrowing a word they tossed around in creative writing classes all the time.

"As opposed to...?" Jill asked.

"An abstraction," someone said, and everybody laughed again.

"A dog is so specific," the first student—Brooke, not at all a stupid girl, and not a half-bad writer, either—added helpfully.

"But we're not talking about poetry," one of the boys said. "We're talking about *life*."

"Indeed," Jill said, at the same time another boy—Marshall, a smart aleck, a charmer, too handsome for his own good—said, "Hell, is there a difference?"

Jessie, who'd been quiet up till then, said, "But what is it supposed to mean, to call something 'specific' in life? When we say something's 'concrete and specific' in a poem in workshop, we always mean it as a *compliment*."

Indeed, Jill thought, but this time she didn't speak.

Brooke answered instead. "What *I* meant is mundane. Part of the ordinary, everyday world."

That presumably Professor J. T. Rosen did not live in.

"Earthbound," Marshall added, and Brooke nodded, "Yes, *exactly*. Earthbound."

Phil, earthbound? Ah, they should see him fly, dragging her along behind him, every night at midnight.

SHE COULDN'T WRITE. She finished out the teaching week and for the next four days at home—Thursday through Sunday—she tried and failed to write. She moved from room to room, carrying her notebook, from her study to the kitchen (where she discovered Phil asleep under the table), to the bedroom, to the living room (where Phil followed her and went to sleep in the bergère).

On Sunday morning she tried to work in the living room, sitting with her feet stretched out straight in front of her on the méridienne, but got nowhere. Phil slept in the bergère, across from her, as usual. That she had allowed the dog to claim this chair was a sign, early on, of the depth of her attachment to him. When he had made plain his partiality to it, all she'd asked of him in return was that he leave the pink méridienne to her. "That's mine," she had explained, on his third day with her. She sat down on the méridienne, to demonstrate. "This is raw silk, and it cost a fortune. I had to buy it myself and send it to North Carolina, and it is *very* delicate, this fabric. Understood?" He'd looked at her gravely. "And it is *my* favorite place to sit. So this one is off limits, got it?" *Yes*, his grave look said, *I understand. Yours.*

After a while she gave up trying to write and went upstairs to the bedroom, where she set down her notebook and read Roth in bed for two hours. Then she went down to the kitchen, carrying *The Counterlife* as well as her pen and notebook, and ate a bowl of lentil soup. Next she drifted to her study, where she found Phil chewing dreamily on a soft rubber hamburger in her reading chair. She sat at her desk and turned on her computer—she never composed on the computer; still, it was worth a try—but she found herself thinking about the men who had passed through her life. So quickly passed through, most of them, as if she were a sieve, as if the men were sand too fine to be caught up in the pan, would run through with the water. Panning for gold, she thought, but there was no gold, only fine gold dust that ran right through the mesh.

How could she write when there was all this clutter in her mind? And this had all started because of thinking of Philip, hadn't it, she thought resentfully —and then of David, too, and all the others, one leading to another. Now she found herself thinking of the newspaper reporter, Leo—no, Leon—and the bass player. Len? Ben? Was she really forgetting names? She couldn't believe it. Had so much time passed, after all?

Well, it wasn't as if she had wasted any of the time that *had* passed thinking of them. But now—here they were, all of them. The artists, three of them. Ken, the abstract painter...and it was true, she realized, she'd forgotten the names of the other two. But then came the actors, one after another. And the playwright—Rich, or Rick. The many poets besides Philip the first. Marco, Roy—but it made her cringe to think of these two and so she stopped there. The musicians—after Len or Ben there'd been a drummer. Robert. Then a trumpet player. Frank? Franklin.

All the men who had slipped through her life,

leaving nothing solid behind.

SHE LOOKED UP Bill's number in the phone book. She hadn't put it in her address book, hadn't imagined that she'd ever need it.

"Bill," she said. "This is Jill—the woman who took that puppy, Dog?"

"Which Dog?" Bill said. Then, "Wait, I know. The brindle pup, right? You're the teacher."

"That's me."

"So how is he? Dog?"

"Phil," Jill said.

"Bill," Bill corrected her.

"No," she said, "that's the dog's name—Phil."

"Oh," Bill said. "Sorry. Well, that's a good name. Phil."

This pleased her so much, she was ashamed.

"So how's it going, then? The dog—Phil—he's all right?"

"He's fine," Jill said. "Everything's fine."

"Well, that's good. I'm sure glad to hear it."

"I thought you might want to know."

"Well, sure. Nice of you to call."

"All right, then," Jill said. "I just wanted to let you know." She was about to say, "Thanks again for everything"—she had worked this out in advance, a polite bridge to "goodbye"—when Bill cleared his throat.

"You know, I've got to tell you. It's funny, but I've thought about that dog. The brindle. I never think about the fosters once I find homes for them. I've trained myself that way, I guess. You'd go crazy if you got too fond of them. I'm careful. But this one—I don't know, like I say, I've had him on my mind. I've even thought once or twice I should've just kept him myself."

"Why?" Jill said. "Why'd you think that, Bill?" Her heart was racing—just like that, it had started pounding hard and speeding up. She felt it whamming in her chest. *Bang, bang, bang.*

"Why?" He seemed to be seriously thinking about the question. Then he let out one of his folksy little chuckles. "I don't know"—she was disappointed that he didn't say "I don't *rightly* know," which she could hate him for—and then, "I guess…he just seemed like such a good dog."

"Good how?"

"Good *how*?" Bill chuckled again. "You ask a lot of hard questions, don't you? Must be because you're a teacher, huh?"

"Possibly."

"Don't know how to answer that one, though. Guess I'd get an 'F' in your class. Be left back." Chuckling, sighing. Some other sound she couldn't even name—a snort or a growl. Possibly he was just blowing his nose.

"What does it mean, 'good'? That's what I'm wondering."

"What's a good dog? That's what you're asking me?" He sounded amazed. "It's just a thing you know about a dog. If you know dogs at all, you know it when you see it."

"And this is something you saw in my dog. In Phil."

"Well…yeah. I run across a lot of smart dogs,

dogs you can tell are going to be real protective, loyal. Some that are easy to train. And then I see a lot of doofusses too. Not that doofusses can't be good dogs in their own way. But this dog—your dog, I could tell, he had a real personality, he was real smart. Extra-smart. Like, sort of a wise dog. Just a little puppy and you could've sworn he understood things. He was just real alert, I guess. You know what I mean?"

"I do."

"Well, sure you do. He's your dog."

Jill closed her eyes. She leaned against the wall where she was standing, in the kitchen. Phil was on the floor, under the table. She knew he was watching her.

"I've got to go now, Bill."

"Well, you take care, then," he said.

"You too."

"And take care of that good dog. Phil, right? That's a good name."

When she hung up she was crying again.

This is getting to be a regular thing, she

thought.

But there were worse things. Plenty of things worse than crying.

THAT NIGHT. A gorgeous night, the sky huge around her in a way she could not recall it ever being at home. At "home," where she had not lived for almost a decade now. Where the night sky was a backdrop, blankly distant, patches of it visible—a rectangle here, a sliver there—looking like a set of empty places waiting to be filled.

Here, tonight, the black sky struck her for the first time in her life not as an absence but as something palpably, colossally present. Stars were strewn across it as if they'd just been shaken and cast and any minute now the way they'd landed would be read aloud to her in a hushed, thrilling voice. She walked under it, this spread of black and silver, feeling graced. She bowed her head. Phil tugged her forward, and above her, all around her, she felt her fortune waiting to be told.

The March wind slapped her face, but softly—like a small cold hand, a child's hand. She had the feeling that everything was soft tonight, and kindly disposed toward her. Even the sidewalk under her feet, under the synthetic "leather" clogs, felt soft, as if it were giving way under every one of her steps.

The trees she passed as she and Phil jogged down the street, street after street, seemed to curve a little toward them. Bowing to us, she thought, and grinned into the soft cold that whipped across her cheeks. She felt something like happy—happy in a small but throbbing, slightly shocking way. As if something were living inside her, small and full and pulsing, unexpected.

What the hell am I doing here? she used to think. She'd ask herself this all the time, whenever she allowed herself to think about the fact that she was here at all. But tonight she felt strangely loving toward this place, this nowhere city, the Midwestern town that had adopted her, the earth itself that had spun and cast her here—by accident!—and full of love for the black and scattered silver of the velvety sky around her, the trees she didn't know the names of but that were paying tribute to her anyway, the houses looking so sweet and so somber and so steady behind their front porches, porch swing after porch swing swaying just a little as if ghosts were sitting there and watching as she flew by with Phil, smiling at the two of them—the houses and the ghosts in their porch swings looking as if they'd been where they were for a thousand, for a million years. She loved the dark windows and the silence that was settled over every house she passed as if they'd all been put under a magic spell. And she loved the sound of her own footsteps, rubber slapping the cement, loved the jangle of Phil's tags against each other—the brand-new teardrop-shaped rabies tag and the registration tag, a gold cloverleaf, that had arrived in the mail a few days after she had brought Phil home and sent in his licensing fee, making him official (she'd clasped the gold tag to his collar and told him solemnly, "Now you are a dog"), sandwiching the heart-shaped red one she'd watched a machine make in the pet store on the day she had gone shopping for him for the first time, Bill's list in her pocket, Phil in his hand-me-down, cheap nylon collar and pulled by a rope. She'd picked Phil up and held him like a baby in her arms while the tiny hammers carved out his name—his brand-new name—and, under that, hers: PHILLIP and J.T. ROSEN, and then her address and phone numbers, home and office both, in case (and already, even then—on day one!—her eyes filled at the thought of it) he was ever lost.

That first night with Phil, she had lain awake thinking of him on the street alone, unwanted, the weeks of wandering. How had he eaten? Stayed warm? The cold, the fear, the loneliness, the hunger and thirst—how had he survived it all to be with her now? To be sleeping peacefully, trustingly, in her arms, sleeping in a bed for the first time in his life, warm enough, with softness all around him? She thought of how when she had taken him away from Bill's house, he had not whimpered, had not looked back, had not expressed even the most fleeting grief or dread, neither over leaving the only home he'd known—the closest he'd yet come to having any sort of home at all—nor over what might lie ahead for him. He had gone from misery to misery—homeless and motherless, wandering the streets, to the clamor and sorrow and at last hopelessness of the pound, to his rescue by Bill, snatched from death only to be set once more, however gently this time, in a cage—and yet he seemed confident that what was ahead was *good*, was not to be feared at all.

He was a dog with faith, an optimistic dog.

What would it mean, she wondered, to imagine that what was good *was* ahead? What would it mean to imagine what was good? To be sure what goodness was. To be sure goodness, whatever goodness was, was possible.

What did it mean to be "sure" something was "possible"?

She wondered, looking down at the dog as he paused on their way home—they were on their own corner, just four houses away from theirs—and took his time to study a recycling bin full of well-washed jars and cans and neatly stacked and rope-tied copies of *The Herald-Tidings-Messenger.* Phil glanced up at her: *Nothing of interest here. Mind if I nose around beside it?* She nodded, both grateful and abashed that for once he had looked to her for her permission. That he understood that her permission was not to be taken for granted—not always.

She thought again now of Philip the first, and wondered—wondered for the first time in all these years!—if she might have overlooked something in him. In him and in all the rest of them. Some potential for goodness—some potential unmet, yes, unmet, unrisen to; but still within them, *possible.* What did it take to tap that possible, that unmet potential, that hidden, deeply hidden, untouched core of goodness?

It could happen by accident; it could happen in the blink of an eye—it could happen *because* you happened to be looking in that direction, just then. Because you knew enough to happen to be looking for it.

Phil dug his nose deep into the softened dirt—the ground was thawing everywhere now, and although it might still freeze again, it wouldn't be long now before the cold would be behind them for the year, before she could shed her jacket and her foolish hat, and everything would be abloom—and as she watched her dog, it struck her that although she might have come upon him accidentally, he had ended up with her *because* of his trust and his faith, which had kept him alive and ready, always, to find that what was ahead would not be more of what was behind him.

She stood looking at the row of sober little houses with their darkened windows, only one—the fourth one from the corner, *hers*—lit up from inside: the only one that looked inhabited, and yet it was likely that it was the only one that was *not* at this moment inhabited. An irony, she thought. The sort of irony she had often (too often?) shaped a poem around.

Life was composed of accidents. It was one accident after another. A single life itself was accidental—a confluence of genetic material that had never before and never would again be possible. An instant earlier, an instant later, and one would have another life entirely.

A series of accidents. Accidents, and reactions to each accident—that was what made a life what it was.

She remembered that her brother had insisted that the affair with his student had come about "by accident." *Oh, yes,* she'd thought but hadn't said, *and what kind of accident would that be?* She'd made a feeble joke about collisions, car crashes, insurance, something like that—which she now regretted, although she could not recall exactly what it was she'd said. Or rather, written. They had "talked" about this only over e-mail. On the phone they were always stiff with each other, kept each other at a distance like the distance that separated their two cities, both of them so far from "home."

She'd made a joke because she hadn't wanted to hear any of the details he seemed so determined to reveal. Perhaps he had told no one else—perhaps that was why he was so eager to tell her what she didn't want to know. She had put him off with jokes, had asked no questions. She didn't know how he'd worked it out in the end—how he'd worked out the rest of his life. He hadn't left Marian, that was all she knew. She had no idea if he had ever *told* Marian. If he'd ever told anyone but her.

Now she was sorry that she hadn't let him talk, hadn't asked him anything, had doubted and even mocked him for using the word *accident*.

One could only plan and account for so much.

She would call Norman tomorrow, she decided. They hadn't spoken since the holidays, when she'd called on Christmas Eve to say Merry Christmas to his children, who were being raised half-Christian. She'd sent them Chanukah presents although she wasn't sure they were celebrating Chanukah (she wasn't a celebrant herself, but it seemed the right thing to do: to point out to them that their father's family was Jewish, after all) and she had not been sure exactly when Chanukah had fallen this year. She had simply sent the presents at the end of the first week of December, wrapped in blue and silver paper speckled with tiny stars of David. She barely knew her nieces and nephew and she had not known what to send, so she sent too much—board games, puzzles, craft kits, stuffed animals she wasn't sure were appropriate for children of their ages. The toy store had wrapped the presents for her, after asking "which holiday" they were for, which impressed her, and stuck a *dreydl* sticker on each one. They'd even shipped the box for her.

Norman would be surprised, no doubt, to learn that she had taken in a puppy. She should invite him—him and his family—to visit. Phil would enjoy that, wouldn't he? And the children would. And perhaps she would, too. It was hard to say.

But certainly she should make an effort to be closer to Norman and his family. And she should make an effort to be more tolerant, more forgiving, of her mother—though perhaps this was asking too much of herself.

A joke—only a joke. She should, could, make an *effort,* at least.

An effort to be closer to Norman and if not to Marian, who had never liked her, then to the children, Joshua and Amy and Jacquelyn. An effort to stop drinking wine for good. An effort to be kinder to her mother, who was after all alone too.

Not *too*. She had Phil, she protested to herself. Who was "just" a dog—so her mother would say, certainly, testing her new forbearance—but who had nonetheless altered her life so that she was *not* alone, in fact. She did not feel alone.

She stood on her corner thinking about the loneliness that had dogged her all her life until she had trained herself to live with it, to be alone without loneliness, not to rise above her loneliness so much as to swim with it, to swim *in* it, to accept it as her medium. It was only then that she had stopped hoping to be lifted from it, stopped wishing to be free of it. She would never be free.

Phil moved on from the soft dirt near the curb and was sniffing hard along the sidewalk edging it. "What do you smell, Phil?" she asked. "What is it, boy?"

They walked slowly, side by side, Phil's nose to the ground. Perhaps he smelled that spring was coming. He didn't know what it was—he couldn't possibly imagine it—but there must be notice of it in the air, on the ground, everywhere around him. Clues that it was coming—that something new was ahead.

She could see him racing through a field, over soft grass, leaping into the air, sniffing at it in wonder. And herself holding on for dear life behind him.

It was a sort of miracle, she thought, that this puppy would be safe and alive in the spring. And that she would be racing behind him—that too.

He had come to her by a sort of accident, yes, but like so many accidents it was one that had needed to happen. It wasn't so much that having Phil had freed her; it was that Phil was swimming by her side.

Or just ahead. There was a hard yank on his end of the leash as Phil sprang into movement suddenly, and in the wrong direction. Jill was startled into laughter.

"Phil! Stop! We were going home, remember? Look, here's our house!"

But he was off and running, pulling her so hard

she leapt—she left the ground. She landed running, and she just kept going. She didn't even try to hold him back. She ran.

acknowledgments

It is with the deepest gratitude that I acknowledge the help (in the form of questions it never occurred to me to ask, mirrors held up to my blind spots, coaxing and exhortations, and the occasional brisk lecture) of M. V. Clayton, whose friendship and editorial ferocity have helped to shape my life as well as my work for nearly thirty years; my comrade-in-arms Erin McGraw, without whom I simply couldn't *do*; Jim Phelan, possibly the best academic colleague a writer could ever hope to have; Lee Martin, who sees the big picture, always, when somehow I cannot; and my wise, stern friend and mentor Lore Segal. And it is with particular pleasure—indescribable pleasure—that I offer my public thanks to Mary Tabor and Nancy Ginzer—once my students, now among my most trusted readers and friends.

I am also indebted—once more, as ever, always—to Marian Young and to my parents, Morton and Sheila Herman. To Grace Jane Herman Holland, my cheering section, chorus, frequent editorial advisor, and sounding board. To Randy Fuller for his enthusiasm and alacrity. And to my very smart young fairy godmother, Kate Nitze.

I owe debts of gratitude too to two institutions that I am glad to acknowledge: the College of Humanities of the Ohio State University and the Greater Columbus Arts Council, both of which provided crucial support when I needed it most.

Finally, I would be remiss not to offer up my thanks—my flimsy verbal *human* thanks—to the fine dog who inspired this story: Molly, my daughter Grace's beloved rescue puppy, who (Dog among dogs—her own dog, always) has been generous enough to be my devoted friend as well.